~The charred corpse had one ruined arm held high, and it bellowed out a sound a healthy throat could never mimic. Smoke rose from the ground at the things feet. The scout was paralyzed. He looked closer. It wasn't smoke, it was steam. Sickly, pink, steam.

The steam didn't rise from the ground, but from the lungs of the dead that littered the battlefield. The steam started around the charred man's feet, but just as those bodies began to shake and shiver, the mist continued to jet from the reborn screams, radiating out toward the scout.

He forced himself up and ran through the burning pain in his leg, not daring to look behind himself again. He didn't want to be around when his boys started waking up. ~

# DEAD

# OF THE

# UNION

ISBN: 0988572702

eISBN 9780988572706

Cover design by Richard Pierick Smith

Illustrations by Corinne Halbert

Author Photo by Yuan Song

*Any hateful, bigoted, or offensive language found in this book does not reflect the beliefs of the author. It was only used to show the world as it once was.*

Printed in the United States of America

First Mass Market Edition

This book is dedicated to Alisha,
my friends and family, my amazing Kickstarter funders,
and Charles Shaw,
without whom none of this
would have been possible.

# CHAPTER 1

Narcisse could see the half-moon glowering down at him from his hiding place. He had ducked and rolled beneath a fallen moldering stump that smelled like autumn. He cursed the half-moon for its betraying light and he cursed himself for being spotted while stealing the pistol that currently dug into his hip. He heard the hissing voices of the dozen Yankee soldiers creeping through the woods around him. He held his dagger close to his body, covering the polished blade with his black hand to hide it from the men and from the moon.

He begged the Loa for help, but he knew they wouldn't answer; he had nothing to offer in his bag aside from his Freeman Papers and a handful of spell ingredients. The Loa had stopped offering charity after he had crossed them for the last time back in New Orleans.

"That river's too deep to swim. Must be around here someplace."

"Shh!"

Narcisse had stolen the pistol hoping he could sell it in the next town. He had run out of food two days previous and money the week before that. He longed for his shack back in Louisiana.

Things had never been simple or easy for him there, but it had been better than the non-stop running and hiding and begging. The slave hunters trying to put shackles on his proud legs even though he had been born free.

The suspicious eyes of the white folk that followed him wherever he roamed were sharpened to razor slits by the paranoia of the war. The jealousy of slaves, envious and hateful of his freedom, mocking him without saying a word.

He knew he could never go back home. He had betrayed too many, on earth and in the spirit world, to try and chisel out an existence there. Too many spurned women. Too many debts owed. Too many hexes lain. A tomb full of bad decisions. The last of his money had gone toward a handful of jerky and a steam boat ticket bound for St. Louis. If he made it that far, he knew he would be free, at least from the smoldering oppression of the South, a chance to start again, he hoped. To leave the troubles he'd made for himself far behind. To be the only Bokor practicing Voodoo in some new town and swim in the benefits.

Now, under the mossy log, he cursed his choices and damned his luck. His last ten years flashed before him, stirred up by the uncertainty of death. It seemed that the Loa had been working against him every step of the way, even as he grew more and more powerful in the mysteries of Voodoo. Lafitte had warned him about the danger of taking dark paths, but Narcisse hadn't listened. Darkness was all he knew since he saw his father dangling from a tree like some strange fruit.

Narcisse had just celebrated his fourteenth birthday a week before his father died. Little Narcisse blinking in the morning sunlight, standing in the door of their shack on the bayou. His father hadn't woken him up as he did every morning.

Thousands of unnamed crawling things screamed in the wet heat like the swamp was the surface of the sun. The boy's mutt dog was jumping and spinning in mad circles. It was biting at something hanging from the tree closest to the shack, some dripping red thing that Narcisse refused to recognize.

The dog had nipped most of the tough meat from the father's feet. Bone showing, ribbons of flesh hanging loose. Narcisse grabbed the dog and snapped its neck like a chicken's. He threw it into the swamp.

The things of the swamp had quietly sucked the dog below the lumpy green foam of the water by the time Narcisse had climbed the unforgiving magnolia and cut his father down.

Corpses don't land like people do when they fall. They don't prepare for the landing, don't get ready. Narcisse heard every crack and pop when the body hit.

A day later Narcisse decided his father belonged in the swamp, as well.

Narcisse ran out of food a week later. He couldn't stand to live in the house his father built any longer. In a strange rage that his young mind could not explain, he burnt the shack to the ground and set off down the long road to New Orleans while the flames still licked at the night.

An empty stomach can make a man do terrible things. After his third night of wandering the streets, the leftover scraps he snatched from the tables of sidewalk cafes hardly dulling the edge of his hunger, a strange thing popped in his brain. He grew a set of rat eyes, looking for opportunity in every gleam in the darkness and a meal in the smallest savory whiff in the perpetual rot of the bayou.

His first verminous act happened the night of a miserable rainy day that had yielded no scraps. The downpour ceased as the moon rose and Narcisse left his damp alley overhang shivering and hungry and angry at the world.

He wandered the night, finding nothing to eat and not even a penny on the ground. The humidity of the festering swamp made it impossible to dry out and the once welcomed cool breeze of February cut through his thin clothes and pinched his skin like a bitter old woman.

He had become a predator. He was no longer scavenging, but hunting. His eyes changed, his walk changed, even his smile changed, twisting from something that had once been natural and welcoming to a show of sharp bone.

At around one o'clock, by the bells of St. Lois cathedral, he had found his prey. On a lonely street Narcisse saw a well-dressed man stumble into an ally to urinate.

Narcisse squeezed into the shadows beside the alley and waited for the drunk's whistling to stop.

He followed as the man weaved through the streets; his wallet poking half-way out of the back pocket of his garish pants like the devil himself had plucked it up in an act of temptation. Narcisse padded silently behind the man, his bare feet making less noise than the runoff in the gutters.

The man tottered along, letting out the occasional mutter or belch, tapping his ill-fitting hat back into place just as it was about to topple to the paving stones. He had no idea the boy was behind him. It was too tantalizing for Narcisse to resist. He imagined the banquet of meat and potatoes he would be able to buy with the cash no doubt bulging from the dandy's pocket. Narcisse cast the last of his morals to the wind. His mind was made up.

His thin fingers reached out, the wallet practically leaping from the drunk's wobbling rear. Closer. Closer.

One last reach to pluck it.

The man stopped without warning and Narcisse's hand dug into his fleshy buttocks. The dark street echoed as both of them yelped in alarm. Narcisse grabbed the wallet a moment before the man spun and grabbed him. The next second was etched into Narcisse's memory, seemingly tattooed on the inside of his eyelids to play before him every night when he tried to go to sleep.

The man bellowed, his face hidden by the shadow of his hat brim. He grabbed the terrified child and shook him as the spittle from his boiling words wet the boy's face. Narcisse clutched the wallet closer to his body and, in his panic, thrust his hand into the man's face. His fingers followed the sloping bridge of the man's nose and skewered into his eyes with a sound that Narcisse tried to forget, but never would. The man released him, screaming loudly enough to send window shutters flying open up and down the street. The boy turned and ran away as fast as his bare feet would let him.

He stopped, blocks away, and hid in an alley behind a barber shop. He remembered it smelled like hair tonic as he shivered behind a pile of crates, chattering sleeplessly all night. He couldn't take his eyes off the empty wallet or his bloody red hand that would not come clean no matter how many times he scrubbed it over the wet cobble stones.

Lafitte found him in the alley the next day, despondent and muttering. The old man took him in and took care of him. In exchange for room and board the boy kept the old man's herb shop clean and ran the errands his old legs could no longer handle. Lafitte tried to teach the boy the high and right mysteries of Voodoo, but as the boy grew to be a young man it was clear that there was something dark and vengeful rooted in Narcisse that could never be shaken loose by any amount of ceremony and love. He grew into a strong, but troubled, young man. Each year growing another bitter layer on him like the rings of a tree.

Narcisse left Lafitte after an argument that left both of the men bloody and heavy with hexes. Narcisse was seventeen and ready to embark on a life of twists and shadows. It seemed like he was born for it.

Something bit Narcisse's leg. It felt like the ember of a cigar being ground into his skin. He sucked in air with a hiss that set the searching soldiers silent. Narcisse did not cry out, but he desperately wanted to. He bit his tongue to drive the crawling pain in his leg from his mind, but it did little to help. The pain moved up his leg, drawing closer and closer to his crotch. He could feel himself perspiring. The slow, careful boots of the soldiers closing in all around him. It was too dark to see what was biting him. Slowly, he moved his hand down his body and touched his leg, but didn't feel it; he felt the tiny carpet of ants that were conquering him at an obscene pace. Acting with one mind they swarmed over his hand and made their way up his arm, leaving a path of fire in their wake.

"Maybe he broke north?" one of the soldiers asked.

"S'pose he could have, let's try and cut him off by-"

Narcisse screamed when the swarm reached between his legs. He scrabbled from beneath the log, rolling in the wet leaves of the forest floor. He tumbled directly into the surprised feet of a soldier. A dozen rifles pointed at him as he scraped the terrible things from his body.

"Well, *shit*." Muttered the soldier.

# CHAPTER 2

From the farmhouse window the acres of corn looked alive, but they were filled with rot.

In previous years Catherine would have sat in her old rocker on the porch with a bit of mending or a book, but this year she stayed indoors. Everything happened through windows now.

Even though the battles had moved off past the forest and over to the hilly country beyond, she felt safer inside. She could hear the weather vane on the roof whine in the changing wind. She could bolt the door if she wanted, but she didn't bother. No one came around anymore.

She had just finished fixing herself a small supper of corn pone with a bit of bacon, but now that she was done, her appetite had left her. Her hands had just made the meal out of habit. She had started measuring enough cornmeal into the bowl to feed four people, then laughed bitterly and scooped most of it back into the sack.

She left the meal on the table, left the kitchen and walked into the front room. Most of the windows in the house were covered, bathing the whole place in a gloom she could almost smell. The furniture was starting to get dusty with no one to use it. There were permanent shadows on the walls left from where she had taken down things she no longer found necessary.

She adjusted the angle of a well-worn wing-chair, stood staring at it for a moment, and then moved it back to where it had been before.

She thought about dusting, then sighed and walked back into the kitchen.

She looked at her cooling plate on the table and sniffed. Nothing but corn for the last week, she couldn't smell it anymore. Couldn't taste it. She sat at the table, the scrape of the chair over the rough wood floor seeming incredibly loud compared to the complete stillness of the house.

She pushed her plate back and poured a cup of water from a chipped pitcher. Her hand dug for the small blue bottle in her apron and she frowned at it as the sky through the window turned from orange to crimson with the setting sun. Written in a small precise hand on the label was, 'Laudanum: five drops for sleep or headache'.

Ten drops fell into her cup and she drank it all down in one slow gulp. She covered the plate of food with a dishcloth and set it in an empty cupboard, then looked at what was outside the window and cleared her throat. She pressed her hand into the small of her back and kneaded the knotty muscles. The digging had kindled a tension there that refused to leave. She was far too old to have dug as much as she had.

Sighing, she walked slowly through the front room and up the stairs. She stood before the first door on the landing and placed two fingers on the doorknob. Her chin sank to her chest. She breathed in and, for an amount of time that would have made a casual observer anxious, held it. When she exhaled, she turned the knob.

The door stuck until she nudged it open with her knee, it let loose with a sound like joints popping. The window was uncovered and the setting sun shone in. The small sweep of the door excited the skin of dust the room had grown since she had last set foot in it. Catherine stood and watched the motes catch fire in the slant of sun through the window.

"Hasn't even been that long." She said.

Everything was as she had left it. The bed was there, stripped to the mattress. The things under the bed she didn't want to think about. The blood stains and the smell that still lingered in the air.

She could still hear the screams, the crying.

Why would god allow such a thing to happen?

It took her only a moment to recollect her lifelong punishment for some ethereal sin that she could not recall. Life and punishment were the same. Happiness was only the temporary respite from the punishment for her.

She felt in her apron pocket and withdrew the pretty purple bottle. Counted five drops onto her dry tongue.

She wasn't sure why she came into the room. She didn't need anything from it. She had felt a call of sorts, as happened when the warm waves of the laudanum started massaging her abdomen. The drawers were too loud when she pulled. All the things were exactly where she had left them, no change. She took a doll from under a stack of unused diapers and slammed the drawer shut.

She could still hear them.

"Quiet! Please, please- *quiet!*" She screamed.

There was a diaper, disheveled and sticking out of the drawer where she slammed it.

Almost waving.

Dizziness washed over her with the pulse of her heart and she fell back against the door jamb.

She could still hear them. The hallway shook as she slammed the door to the dusty room. The bassinet within swung on its fresh hinges. Then she was outside, in the yard. Her toes were just touching the mound of the fresh grave. She placed the old doll into the brass vase she had half buried there.

"I miss you."

She sniffed and stood up straight. Her back still hurt from the digging. Behind her the weathercock screeched once and pointed south.

She sat down at the table and poured herself another cup of water. Five more drops dissolved into it like they were nothing at all. She drank it and went to the closet. Took out the shotgun. Made sure it was loaded. Threw out supper. Washed the dishes. Brought the gun with her up the stairs to her own room. She didn't say her prayers that night.

# CHAPTER 3

Hiram had hung about the general's tent like a five o'clock shadow for most of the day, trying to act like he belonged there, which he didn't. A sharp shooter had no business in the area, the narrowness of the alley between rusty brown tent rows kept him out of sight, but being spotted there would require a series of lies that would be epic in magnitude.

The general hadn't left his tent in days, giving Hiram no chance to sneak in and spirit away any maps or plans. He had a week until his next check in with a Rebel contact; he had been told at his last meeting that if he didn't provide any information soon bad things would happen to him.

Being an unwilling spy was the worst position Hiram could imagine during wartime, asides from being a casualty. Though, sometimes he envied both the crippled and the dead.

He thought bitterly about how he had landed in this morass. A double agent, a liar, a cheater. A condemned man who could have nothing to look forward to but a noose or a firing squad. The saloon was filled with conscripted CSA boys. Jensen's Regulars had mustered in Texarkana the previous week and today was their big payoff. The heaven that came before their hell was the one hundred fifty dollar bounty they received for enlisting. They had gotten it that morning from a well-guarded little man with a strongbox, and those that didn't have families to send it to, or didn't care to, were living high hog the few precious days they had before gun-smoke and mud would be all they knew.

Hiram had been unexpectedly successful on his last spying mission for the Union. He played the role of a simple infantryman to General Staunton's troops.

He got close to the general, eventually becoming a regular guard of his quarters after gaining the general's trust through a series of lies about a shared hometown.

One night, a week before a massive offensive was planned to occur, Hiram had snuck into the general's tent as he slept and sketched the battle plans into his bible by lamp light. He slipped into the night and days later met his Union contact. The rough map and timetable he stole was enough to cause a number of crushing blows against the CSA.

Hiram knew that it didn't matter who was winning in a war, good men would always die no matter the victor, but the blood clotted heavy on his hands from those slaughtered in the string of surprise attacks. There was one constant state for Hiram; in success and failure, in virtue and sin, there was always guilt. He had done so well on this mission, the Pinkerton Detective Agency sent him right back into the maelstrom.

Now he was Jonathan Gurnsey, or Little John as his fellow Confederates called him. A halfwit from Washington, Arkansas, that was afraid of the dark but could sharpen any piece of steel you put in his hand until you could shave the thickest beard with it.

He sat in the corner of the saloon, playing his part, sipping his whiskey and sharpening a wicked Arkansas Toothpick so he would be left alone, as large men with knives often are. Occasionally he would take the edge of the dagger to his forearm and shear a patch of hair baby smooth just to prove a point.

A well-dressed man with an impeccably tended Van Dyke appeared in the bar with two heavy set friends. They bore no uniform or rank and appeared as natural in the sawdust saloon as a hornet in a pitcher of lemonade.

The mustachioed man wandered to the bar and ordered a drink. His friends seemed happy to linger on either side of the only exit. Hiram noticed all of this while trying to appear that he hadn't.

He tugged the bill of his cap low over his eyes and focused intently on the whetstone. His fears were proven when the mysterious man lifted the tails of his coat and sat down on the stool across the little table from him. Hiram examined the blade closely while letting his free hand wander to the pistol at his side. The man spoke with a refined Atlanta drawl.

"I'd just go ahead and leave that sidearm be, seeing as I've already drawn on you."

There was a muted click beneath the table.

As he'd done so often before stepping on stage, Hiram shuffled his facial features to the part he was playing. He looked up from the blade with glassy unfocused eyes, jaw slack, lower lip hanging lazily.

"Who're you, mister? Am I gettin' more money for signin' that paper?"

"You can drop the ruse, Hiram. I know who you are," He nodded to the two men by the door. "*We* know who you are."

Hiram's face tightened back up and he frowned.

"That's some terrible luck, haven't even started my first mission and already I'm caught." Hiram shook his head sadly.

"Oh *my*, you are a slick willy, aren't you? You and I both know this isn't your *first* run around the track. Let's talk like gentlemen, now, and put down that *barbaric* hunk of steel, hm?"

The perfect mustache curled up in a way that made Hiram want to smack it off of his face. He placed the dagger on the table and met the man's eye. The man was painfully familiar, but he could not track down were he had seen those eyes. Hiram tried to hold a poker face while he replied.

"Who are you?"

A small twinkle of surprise flashed in the man's eyes when he heard the question, then passed.

"You can call me Mr. Doughty. Counter intelligence officer in the Signal Bureau of these Confederate States. Pleased to meet you."

"Wish I could say the same."

"Come *on*, Hiram," Doughty's mustache twisted up in an amiable smile, "You should try to be a *touch* more pleasant seeing as I could have had you killed any number of times in the last week." He took a sip of his drink and chuckled effeminately.

"Why, I could out you as a spy here and now and let these fine men do with you what they will."

Hiram cast an uneasy glance about the burly crowd. Already there were suspicious eyes peering over brown bottles at the dandy and the idiot talking in the corner. Like so many men, they were always on the lookout for the smallest excuse to kill.

"Well then, sir, why haven't you done so?"

"The story is this; I'm a kind and *gentle* man." He took another sip of his drink and relaxed back on the stool. "I've always preferred making friends over enemies, and I've never relished extinguishing another man's *life*."

That last sentence stirred something within Hiram and he hid his revelation behind his whiskey glass. Word for word it had been a line from a play in which Hiram had a secondary role, before the war. The man across from him had been the star. Hiram had tried out for the lead role. The man across from him now had won it. It appeared he had been bested again. He ground his teeth.

"What do you want from me?" Hiram wanted to punch the smug little mustache off Doughty's face, though that wasn't his name. What had it been?

"I merely wanted to offer you a choice, you can either do a few odd jobs for us, or, *well*, the other option is rather, *unpleasant*." Doughty smirked and finished his drink. "But we shouldn't talk much more here, before I tell you any more, I'm going to need to know your choice."

He extended his hand. "What do you say?"

Hiram took his hand and pumped it twice.

"I hope your bureau has better whiskey than this swill."

Hiram was brought through the merry streets to the back office of an unassuming print-shop. The place had proofs of posters tacked up, covering every spare inch of wall space.

There were recruiting posters, beckoning young men to join the fight for the freedom of sovereign southern ideals and promising princely bounties. Hiram noted that any one of the posters could be changed to one boosting the Union by changing only a few choice words. A toothsome whiskey was poured for both of them and, without any further pleasantries; Doughty opened a fat ledger and began paging through it. It was filled with silver prints, sketches, newspaper clippings, and folded maps. Doughty plucked one of the maps from its pocket and carefully flattened it over the worn green blotter of the desk. He cranked up the wick on the desk lamp and pointed to an 'X' that had been drawn in Mississippi.

"I do hope you understand that I'm only going to tell you the bare-bones of what you need to know for this mission."

Hiram nodded, not taking his eyes off the map. He felt as though a specter was playing his spine like a harp.

"Union forces under General Wrathbone have pushed into Mississippi, but our current scouting shows them moving North once more, we assume to block an assault that we are currently mustering."

Hiram tilted his head.

"An attack of which you need to know very little."

Hiram drummed his fingers on the oily old oak of the desk and blew air through his mustache.

"We shall give you this; fifty dollars in both Union and Confederate cash, a uniform matching your assumed rank as well as authentic papers listing you as a sharpshooter from Illinois. Are you handy with a rifle, *by the by*?"

Hiram nodded. "I can shoot the head from a match at a hundred yards."

Doughty slapped the desk and laughed, "Ah hah! Getting into character already. Marksmen are indeed the worst kind of braggart."

Hiram made a noise like a horse and finished his whiskey.

The rest of the details were laid down as Hiram became more and more sober. There was a network of spies in every town of consequence. He was given a sheaf of innocent looking letters from 'home' in which were hidden the names and locations of agents he was to contact at regular intervals. If he did not check in for a month he would be listed as a blackguard and disposed of immediately.

"Mind you, our agents are everywhere and can be anyone. So, if you were thinking of high-tailing it to the territories you may just find your grocer has mixed arsenic in your oatmeal." As Doughty put it.

The next week Hiram had infiltrated Wrathbone's battalion and they swallowed his story whole. Soon he was starving next to his fellow Union countrymen as they marched to Kentucky. When they passed through towns he dutifully reported to his Signal Bureau contacts, brothel girls more often than not.

He didn't make any friends among the Union soldiers as he was certain that the information he leaked was the handle to the scythe that would soon mow them all down. It was one thing to watch a stranger die; it was another all together to watch a friend. Some small part of Hiram was waiting for that blade, even begging for it.

\* \* \*

General Wrathbone was a hard-case, to be sure. On previous assignments Hiram had been able to get close to his targets easily, one of the many reasons he made such a good spy. He would buddy up with the generals and earn their confidence, only to take what he needed and disappear into the night.

Wrathbone only spoke to a small circle of officers, and though he uncannily remembered the names of every enlisted man under his command, he rarely spoke to them. The handful of times Hiram had attempted to make the acquaintance of the general he was stiffly rebuffed, the general letting him know that he knew who Hiram was and that he didn't have any time to waste on him.

So it came that Hiram had to use simple skullduggery in place of intrigue. As a sharpshooter he had a fair amount of down time between missions, though that was rapidly dwindling as with the sour turn the battle had been taking. He had found an alternative to sneaking in the front of the command tent. There was a seam at the back in the alley it shared with a dozen other officer tents. The seam was only two feet high, a rip that had obviously been mended hastily by a soldier that knew as much about sewing as he did the bottom of the ocean. It had been stitched with a rough uneven zigzag with what looked to be a boot lace. A single snip at the top of the repair would cause the whole thing to open up with ease.

Hiram gave up his vigil at the ringing of the lunch bell. If he had the choice, he would have skipped the meal; since supplies were cut off they had only been handing out rations of hard tack chased with a ladle of soup that could hardly be called more than salty water. He couldn't miss it though; this was when the commanding officers did the afternoon headcount. All of his hard work to gain the trust of the Union army would be lost if he were listed as AWOL.

He cut through the camp, weaving past hobbling wounded soldiers, destined for the rear of the food line. He dodged an odd crater, blasted by an enemy shell that had found the perfect trajectory and lofted over the hill that protected the camp, landing towards the rear near the officer's tents. Quartermaster Killers, the enlisted boys called them.

The drum beat of cannon blasts and rifle shots echoed fiercely in the distance. The muscles in Hiram's back stiffened. Anxiety had found a home in Hiram, and he feared it would never leave.

In the last week he and the rest of the sharpshooters had been sent out on missions nine times. They had lost four of the original twelve one by one to opposing marksmen and shrapnel. Every soldier thought he had the worst job, no matter what his specialty or rank, but the sharpshooters had it particularly bad.

Most of the enlisted men would chuckle at the mention of the sharpshooters. It was imagined that they would simply wander to a grassy hill far from the battlefield, hunker down and take pot shots at the enemy at their leisure. The reality was altogether different.

When the marksmen were given orders they set out at a fast march, cutting through any and all rough territory to make sure they arrived before their window of opportunity clapped shut.

They would march miles out of the way, circling the battle field so that a clear view of the enemy lines could be had. The scout that had come before them would let them know where their targets were, usually officers or artillery emplacements. If they took too long, which seemed to be the case half of the time, the target would have moved and the trip would have been for nothing.

Even if the unit arrived with time to spare, it was a deadly game. They would fan out; hide themselves as best they could, aim, fire, run. The second they opened fire, they exposed their position and had to move before the hellfire rained down. The telltale muzzle flash and puff of powder-smoke may as well have been a fuchsia handkerchief waved coyly at the enemy.

They would fire and run, over and over, until the captain decided it had become too dangerous to continue, which as a rule happened after three men had been wounded or one had died. They did not think highly of their captain.

They called him 'Father Death' behind his back. They still respected him and his orders, more out of fear than anything else. He was the best shot any of them had ever seen and carried more lead in him than a tackle box.

Hiram stood in the bread line, shuffling along with the mass of dusty men. He had the little box of ammunition clipped to his belt open; he counted the number of bullets it contained with the touch of his fingers. His eyes were straight ahead, burrowing into the rings of dirt round the neck of the man ahead of him. The box was full.

"Four rows of ten, forty dead men." He said to no one at all.

The other men bantered in the line. Hiram kept to himself as he was not in the habit of keeping the company of dead men. More and more as the war progressed; he realized they were all dead men, himself included. Bullet or blade, hunger or rot, all the enlisted had a foot in the grave the second they leave their cot.

"It's an interesting new stink they're serving us today." Said the soldier behind Hiram.

"You suppose it's a boot, or a tasty knot of horsehair they've dropped into the soup today?"

"Close, I hear tell a mule gave up the ghost and the cookies had their way with it."

"You don't say?"

"There's a teamster that's powerful angry. Heard him say he wouldn't have any of it. Said he brought the beast from his own farm, had it named and all."

"Shame, shame. I'll offer my condolences once I've had some lunch. Haven't had a bite of meat for a week, save for chewing on my lips."

Hiram sat soon after with the rest of the sharpshooters, sipping at tin cups of the mule broth, softening up shingles of hardtack before attacking the big bland crackers with their strongest teeth.

"We're gonna get sent out today." Hobb said into his cup as he sipped. He was the oldest of the group, his salt and pepper mustache was so long it obscured his mouth and gave his voice a curious buzz.

"Who told you that?" Said a wiry, sooty-haired recruit, a bit too loudly.

"Nobody. Just got a feelin'." He massaged a knot at the base of his neck. "Don't think I'm gonna sleep in my bunk tonight."

"Don't go jinxing us, Hobb." Brecht said, his big, watery eyes squinting like he was taking aim. "Just because you're luck is running out doesn't mean you have to pull us down with you."

"Just making a little chin music, Brecht, just sayin' what's on my mind. Have to keep talking to cover up all the awful noises you make when you're eating."

Brecht stopped mid-chew and narrowed his eyes at Hobb, who was peeling at a broken nail. The other men chuckled, making Brecht's face blush up.

"That's right," Said another soldier. "The rebel gunnies don't have to use a glass when they fire the cannons, they just wait for suppertime and aim at the chewing!"

Another dry chuckle shuddered between them.

"Go to hell, all of you." Brecht chewed slowly and deliberately. His head was cocked as though he were trying to hear himself.

They continued ribbing each other. Hiram carefully wrapped his hardtack in a handkerchief and tucked it into his rucksack, with the other portions he had hoarded over the previous days. There was enough to last him a week on the run if he rationed himself harshly.

One by one the men fell silent as the shadow of Father Death fell over them. Hiram felt a chill when the captain's crowfeet circled eyes fell on him.

There was something missing in them, like looking into empty copper pipes. His black goatee looked like it had been painted on, and it hardly moved when he spoke. He used words as though they cost a dollar a piece.

"Meet back here in an hour. We're heading out."

Resigned mutterings made their way around the circle.

"Pack light." The captain looked directly through Hiram when he said this. Hiram was known to carry more than one rifle into combat, the weight making him lag behind the other men.

"Nothing but the Sharps and a song in my heart, sir."

"I pray so, soldier."

The captain turned on his heels and seemed to disappear between blinks of Hiram's eyes.

Hobb finished the last of his soup in a swig and spoke.

"You heard the captain. Grab your prayer-books and your gonads. We're going out."

Brecht flicked his cup with a ting and joked halfheartedly.

"Yeah, Hiram, leave that old shotgun under your pillow, we aren't shooting ducks."

"Brecht, I only hope that one day your mouth is good for better things than drawing flies." Hobb muttered. When Hobb spoke, even quietly, everybody heard. Another soulless chuckle. The laughter had been driven from them after their first kill.

"God damn all of you." Brecht said to his boots.

Hiram drained off the rest of his broth and saw that there was a single chunk of potato clinging to the bottom. He tilted the cup up and tapped the bottom until the morsel came unstuck. It slid into his mouth and he chewed it slowly with relish.

He left the circle before the other men and cut another hasty path to the officer's tents, hoping for one more chance at snatching intelligence. He felt that every mission he had gone on was a throw of the dice. He'd thrown sevens every time so far, and it was only a matter of time before the snake eyes stared up at him, be it a bullet or mortar or ambush.

He had never enjoyed gambling, and the fact that he was forced to do it daily made him bitter. He could already tell that his trip to the rear had been for nothing. The general's slurred voice ripped through the canvas of the tent. It sounded like he had received bad news and was responding like he often did when drunk, the poison spilling from his mouth so hot and vitriolic that it could melt an anvil. Hiram watched silhouettes flicker over the thinner patches of the tent, the overcast sky giving a feeling of night, though it was barely midday.

Hiram gave up and headed back the way he had come. His priorities twisted in his mind. He longed for a day when he wouldn't have to fear death with every decision he made. He hoped that this mission would be his last. He was also afraid of the same thing.

# CHAPTER 4

General Wrathbone could remember when he could taste whisky. Far off in some cloudy hollow in the back of his mind where all the sane and sober thoughts had gone. The only thing he tasted any longer was the coppery tang of his tongue every dry gulch morning, when he awoke with too many voices in his head and the nimble fingers of ghosts plucking at him, drawing him back down into sleep so they could torment him in the quick eternities that lie between drowsy blinks.

A strong cup of coffee fortified by a half dozen glugs from whatever bottle was handy was what it took to put the vengeful spirits to sleep for the day so he could get some work done. So he could return to being a madman.

Before the war, he remembered, drink had brought merriment to his dark world. Spending money. Filling the holes that ran through the heart of his friends and himself with bottles and bottles. Pressing back tomorrow with every burning chug. What had scared him was the emptiness that came with the night, and the great black spot of tomorrow. No plan would ever stick after the black curtain of night had obscured it. This was the only way Wrathbone could live his life; the thought of one long future to plan for terrified him. He worked infinitely better living each day for all it was. The trail of broken glass he left behind him proved this. It made him a terrible husband, but an excellent general.

Just before the war broke out, his Esther had left him. In his endless, empty life she had been the one thing worth living for. He had quit drinking for her, but she had left him sober and alone after sharing the same bed for fifteen years.

She had said he was terrible when he was drunk, but inconsolably sad when he was sober.

After that, the hole had been nearly impossible to fill.

He had fallen asleep at his desk in the command tent once again, the sterile alcohol sweat he produced in his sleep kept his rumpled uniform from smelling in any way human, though he hadn't bathed in nearly a month. He didn't recall the last time it seemed prudent to leave the tent.

His sandy eyes began to focus, and he saw the plans on his desk had been folded by unseen hands and stowed neatly in a valise. The bottles from the previous night were gone as well; he recalled there had been quite a few, even before he had blacked out. They had been replaced with a still steaming cup of coffee, half full, and a dish with two pieces of burnt toast spread with butter and a single beaten raw egg. This was his daily breakfast.

A fresh bottle had also been placed before him. His shaking hands had uncorked it and filled the coffee cup to brimming before he noticed the tidy captain waiting patiently for him, just within the flap of the tent. The general took a lengthy sip before he spoke.

"Can I help you, Captain Goddard?" He set down the cup and took up a piece of the sodden bread. It didn't take much chewing.

The captain stepped to the front of the desk. He saluted and stood at ease without the general commanding it. The captain had built up a kind of quiet insolence in the weeks since they had been pinned down and cut off from supplies. It made the general nervous. He always imagined he heard people hissing just behind his back. A whispering mutiny.

"Good morning, sir. I wanted to get your final word on the offensive you laid out last night." He smiled in a tight little way that made his perfectly trimmed mustache tilt up in just a way that made Wrathbone want to cut it off of him with a hand axe.

"Yes," The general said, his eyes peered down to the desk as if the answer lay somewhere among the runny yolk on his dish. "Of course. Proceed as ordered."

The captain raised an eyebrow.

"Are you sure, sir?"

The general panicked within, but didn't allow it to show. He crammed the overlarge bite of bread into his mouth and chewed slowly, wiping a bit of yolk from his beard with his already stained cuff. No matter how hard he fought, he couldn't remember what orders he had given the night previous. His fear of his own decision dissipated as the slick mouthful slid down his throat. He drank off half of the cup. *Who* were they to second guess his orders? He felt the little button of flesh between his brows tighten and burn like a cigar cinder. He leaped from his seat and slammed his fist on the desk, he was crouched over it as though he would vault it any second and tear out the captain's throat. The bottle wobbled to and fro, but failed to topple.

"I said it and I *meant* it, captain." His fist shook the desk once more. "If you question my orders once more, I'll thrash you until a god damned leper would pity your face."

The captain had retained an erect posture, but melted back to the tent flap in one smooth movement, as though he had practiced it.

"As you wish, sir." The last bit he spat at the ground before he ducked out of the tent like a magician after a botched trick.

Wrathbone was not done. He hollered after the man.

"Yellow bellied gal-boys like you are why we're losing this battle!"

He sat down hard, dragging his nails through the trenches he had already worn in the hickory wood of the desk. At the right angle, they looked like rows in a cornfield. He wanted to take up a great scythe, like death himself, and sunder the enemy with it until they gave up their damned fool ideas and surrendered. Only then could the general finally be left alone, left to his own devices and maybe die unnoticed in a gutter.

Then he could take on the thousands of spiritual reparations he owed to the men he had sent to their death. To finally, hundreds of tear stained years distant, apologize to that last new recruit who hadn't even had the chance to fire his rifle before he was cut down.

The general felt he had a lot of work to do once he was dead, and he knew that every day he spent above ground only meant another eternity of atonement to account for. He had to make the decision he made every morning for the last fortnight. It was the only thing he felt he could do to make his horrible life even with those of the soldiers he cast into the furnace of war every day.

He pushed the dish with its piece of untasted bread to the side and set his sidearm on the desk. He stared at it for a moment, almost imagining it would move by itself, but it was still and cold and gleaming with the terrible kind of unlife that is borne only by knives and guns and teeth. He wanted to finish the drink before he performed his morning ritual, but then he would have nothing to look forward to if he survived.

He took up the revolver and emptied all the chambers but one. With a slap from his palm, the cylinder spun clicking like a cricket held over a flame. A jerk of the wrist snapped the chambers back home. The General's eyes wanted to cheat and look over to see where that one bullet was, but his neck was stronger than the urge. It twisted his head so there was no way for him to know if the fatal chamber was next in line before the hammer. The pistol arced a crescent until the general felt the cool barrel on his temple.

If there was any shaking in his hand, he knew it was not his fractured nerves, but the trembling of the anxious earth beneath his feet. He opened his eyes wide. Only cowards died with their eyes closed. He spoke the only prayer he remembered.

He felt the trigger, greasy beneath his finger. He smelled, for a moment, his own astringent odor. The trigger was no different than any other piece of steel, but it held so much more power.

There was a soul shattering snap, the general felt alive for one swallow-swift moment, but it left him as soon he realized he was not dead.

"One more day." He murmured, dropping the revolver on the desk. He drained what was left in the cup and sucked at the drops of the bitter mixture that clung to his mustache.

"One more day."

The tent seemed to grow dim. He smelled something sour on the wind.

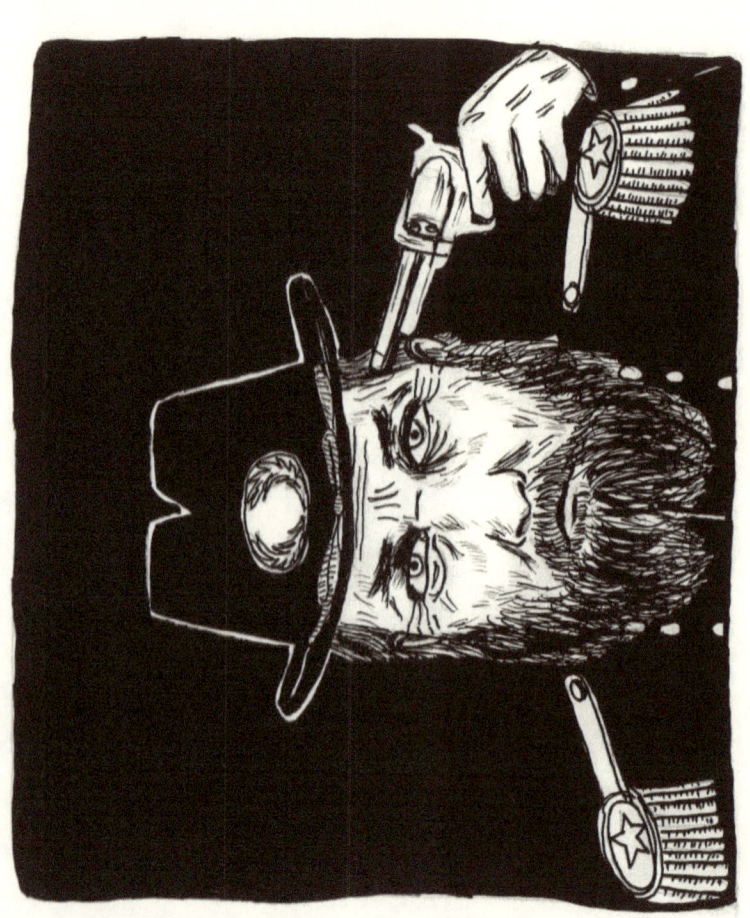

# CHAPTER 5

Declan paced the solitary watchtower overlooking the Union camp with the kind of energy reserved for men that had nothing but a noose to look forward to after supper. The tower had been hastily built, and his heart would rise to his throat every few moments when the wind shifted and he could feel the mess of timber beneath him settle and creak.

He could hear the unopened letter crinkle in his breast pocket with every step. It sounded like a sad, small thing dying.

He thought about his mother as he had left her. Wrinkled and tea-stained just like the letter. Miss McCullough from next door sitting in the squeaky chair next to the forever dying woman's bed, adjusting with a creak every time she turned a page of her tattered and coverless bible. The walls of the building were so thin he could hear the clock an apartment over ticking like a mechanical mouse in the wafer thin plaster. He'd sold his mother's mantle clock to buy a sack of potatoes and a tiny vial of medicine, both of which only made his mother throw up.

She hadn't spoken in the week since he had enlisted. It was a mystery whether she refused to speak or if the disease had taken her tongue. He visited her for a few hours after his shift at the stockyard, still stinking of blood and shivering from the number of souls that had passed through him. He would never sit, just watch her, stand sentinel over her. She, tucked in to too many thin blankets, her head rolling back and forth saying silently 'No, no, no-' with a slowing pace as a dying metronome would.

She looked dry, so he poured a cup of water from the warm pitcher beside her bed and cradled her head. He said;

"Mother, mother, here-"

But her head kept rolling; lips tight like an old wound, her eyes shriveled and small as though they'd seen too much. He was struck with the notion to dash the water on her old face and scream into her ears until she gave up this nonsense. How could anyone be so sick?

He put the cup down and stepped back to his safe distance and held his head, breathing wetly. She had been so strong. He had ridden in her arms, he could remember. The first time he had picked an apple at the long dead family orchard. He could remember. She had held him up and said;

"Reach! Reach, Decky! Tha's the one! Pull! O! An you've got it!"

The damnable ticking of the clock. Feeling that little mouse gnawing within him. Bit, by bit, by bit. The room smelled worse somehow than the killing floor at the stockyards. He left without saying goodbye, knowing she wouldn't hear it.

The stink was on him until he changed into his uniform, but ever since he would fancy it still clung to him. A ghost that would haunt him when the wind blew just so, as it did that day up in the watch tower. Was it the reek of death, or had he always smelled that way?

\* \* \*

He could hear the battle ramping up. He wanted more than anything to be down and away from the noise, but he felt safer in the tower and he would take a tall cage over a field of slaughter. The fog of war was thick past the protecting hill, flashing with powder charges like a sulfurous thunderhead riding the lows of the land.

If the enemy made it up the hill, even Declan in the tower wouldn't see them until it was too late. He gave up watching that front and scanned the camp instead.

It seemed almost still if he didn't focus on any one thing, but the moment he did he could spy little pockets of activity. Nearly as though he was looking at an anthill. A feeling of helplessness washed over him. He watched a mule being slowly led down the main avenue by a teamster. The mule wanted to go everywhere the teamster didn't, causing the man to swear and swat at the beast with his hat.

He reached into his pocket and began to remove the envelope, but he stopped. He sighed as he felt something within himself snap. He never thought he would become such a coward that he would be afraid of the contents of a letter.

Off over in the artillery line one of the cannons disappeared in an explosion of dirt and metal. Half a second later the blast reached his ears, muted with distance. It was followed by a strange humming sound as Declan's eyes traced a black object arcing through the air over the camp. It slammed down onto the main avenue throwing up a hail of clay. In another moment the dust cleared, leaving the teamster in view. He was holding his head as he fell to his knees and sent up a wail that the whole camp could hear. The mule lay in bits around the still steaming cannon barrel that had dug itself into the earth.

Declan reached into his pocket and took out the letter. After one deep breath, he opened it.

# CHAPTER 6

You're the best goddamn tater peeler I ever had, *Narsus*." Said Cookie Todd. "Specially for a coon like you."

The fat man wobbled around the potato covered table and slapped Narcisse on the back, making him drop the potato he had been working on. He laughed. Narcisse winced, but the false grin returned to his face by the time he turned insolently to Todd's round red face and replied.

"Proud to be of service."

"Heh, that's right, Narsus." Todd picked up one of the peeled potatoes and inspected it. "Aw, look here, you missed a- woop!"

He chucked it into the pile on the table, causing half of the clean white tubers to roll off the table and onto the dirt of the floor.

"Aw, shoot. Look at that. Good at peelin', bad at pilin'."

There was a quiet fury in Narcisse, one that he had always carried with him. The little dull knife in his hand shook as the shackles about his ankles rattled. The two weeks since his capture had been like this day in and out. He had learned he was hated universally. It didn't matter north or south. There was no place in between; Mason or Dixon. His skin granted him purgatory, a short knife, and unlimited potatoes.

"You should just go ahead and scrub those off. Don't want the boys getting sick. Us white fellows can't live off of dirt like you folk."

Todd wandered back to his own table, there were two chickens, necks freshly snapped. He dipped the first carcass in a boiling pot to loosen the feathers. Narcisse gritted his teeth and hobbled over to the wash bucket. He hummed to drown out the angry voices in his head while he cleaned the dirty potatoes and set them carefully back in the pile. Todd was an old hand and had the chicken bare in five minutes, slapping it down on the table and dipping the next one.

"Yessir, turns out in order to get a nigger to work, you just got to put the fear of god in his heart and a pair of manacles on his legs." He said, seemingly to himself.

Narcisse stopped scrubbing and glowered up at Todd. The trembling in his body stopped. His rage had passed into something far more terrible. He began calling out with his mind, pulling his threads into the spirit world. Bargaining. Asking small favors. Many little things began happening that no one man would notice.

A sandy haired soldier named Rutherford stood just past the canopy of the cookie's open sided tent. He didn't nod in agreement to the statement, nor did he offer any dissent. He just brought the bill of his cap a bit lower over his eyes and scanned the surroundings for any hungry soldiers looking to steal a proper meal.

Narcisse began to make a noise that was halfway between mumbling and humming. The pupils of his eyes dilated as he scrubbed the last potato clean and set it on the table.

"Stop it with that mumbo jumbo. There'll be plenty of time for you to pray before supper." Todd said over his shoulder. The feathers of the second chicken weren't coming out as easily as they had with the first. Todd dipped it back into the boiling pot to soften it farther. Narcisse continued to stare at the fat man's back.

He took the knife up in his hand. The movement was rock solid and deliberate as clockwork. He dragged the dull blade across the back of his hand. It took two passes before the skin broke and it took a third slash to bring his hot red blood to the surface.

"You crazy pick-a-ninny, I can do that too, who you prayin' to? Your monkey god?" Todd took on a mocking mush mouthed growl.

"Hum jamma mamma boom, monkey monkey-"

Narcisse crept around his work table to the cookie's cutting table where the plucked chicken crookedly laid, a pink pile of limp pimply meat, the head still attached, twisted so it faced backwards and up.

"Oomah looma tippie toe, monkey monkey, doe lay de-"

Todd continued, starting to have fun with it, wiggling his surprisingly small back side. He was all gut and wobbling neck. He didn't see Narcisse, who was safely hidden by the blind spot created by the floppy hat perched on the back of Todd's fat head. Narcisse let blood drip onto the plucked chicken. The drops flowed through the little valleys and fat folds until it almost seemed like they were forming twisted symbols. In a moment he was back at his station wrapping a bit of cloth around his wounded hand.

"Hum la-la lum dah day, heh, heh. Hey boy, think I made your monkey god happy?" He turned back to Narcisse, who was silently peeling potatoes once again.

"Cat got your tongue, boy?"

Narcisse only flashed his white teeth at the cookie.

"Fine by me, stay quiet. Can't understand a damn word you Creole niggers say, anyway."

Todd turned back, pulled the boiling carcass from the pot and, finding the skin had loosened enough, started plucking great stinking handfuls of feathers. He began humming as he worked. He didn't hear what was going on behind him.

The wrong-facing head of the plucked chicken rose up with a series of small pops like corn kernels hitting hot oil. Its claws scrabbled for purchase on the hash-marked wood of the cutting table, soon getting a grip and lifting the flabby body up on thin shaking legs.

A croak crawled from its beak, flapping flatulently through the ruined wind-pipe. The dead bird twitched and skittered on the slick surface, every inch of it jiggling.

One of its claws kicked a swag bellied skinner knife from the table, which landed in the stony dirt with a clatter.

Todd turned and started.

"C- Christ!"

The carcass on the cutting board let out a horrible cry and jumped at the fat man, its bare little wings slapping at its pale sides.

The claws dug into Todd's shirt and held like fish hooks. Its torso jerked back and forth, swinging the head up into the cookie's soft, sweaty neck. Each little peck opening the wound next to his throbbing jugular a bit wider. All the time those little naked wings slapping like an amputee was applauding a show.

Todd struck at the thing like he was swiping at a hornet, but it would not let go. Narcisse stopped peeling, but the smile did not leave his lips. He watched and swayed as though he were moved by unheard drums. Rutherford, just outside the tent, let the butt of his rifle drop to the ground. He watched with a slack jaw and wide eyes. It was uncannily like a nightmare he had had a year before that had put him off chicken for a month.

Narcisse allowed himself a laugh as the fat man spluttered, trying to make some sort of noise, but the sharp pecks at his neck cut him off every time. His striking arms flailed and he stumbled backwards, tripping over his own boot. He reached out on the way down and caught a firm grip on the edge of the boiling pot, sopping feathers still floating on the surface of its dirty brine. The pot came down with him.

Both he and the dead thing on his chest screamed as they were bathed in the boiling putrid water. Todd rolled back and forth over the pecking lump of meat, his scream outlasting his lungs until he was just gasping as a half drowned man would. His already pink skin had blossomed to roses and violets where the water had hit him.

The smell of boiled pork and burning hair turned heads in the acre of surrounding tents.

The big man rolled his bulk on top of the horrible bird one last time and stayed there. His shocked system shut down.

He lay on his belly, jiggling with the slowing shudders of the bird, gasping. Even as he lay on the cool dirt, blisters began to bloom on his face and neck, stripes like badly applied war paint began to stand tall against his exposed pig pink skin. The breaths became labored. His body started spasming.

Two of the assistant cooks arrived from the far side of the camp and dropped their hefty red stained sacks on the cutting table with a meaty plop.

One saw the cookie right away and was silent, mimicking Rutherford's reaction; the other was short and didn't see over the table. He spoke.

"Grand news, Mr. Todd, We've got damn near eighty pounds of meat for tonight! It was mad how it happened..."

He heard the choked breathing and lifted himself to look over the table. He saw.

"Mr. Todd!" He ran to where the shaking man lay. His hands floated about the shivering pile, but refused to touch it.

"Christ! Blazes..." He jumped to his feet.

"Medic!" He shot off down the row of tents with his arms in the air.

"Medic!"

Narcisse continued to smile as he peeled the rest of the potatoes.

Rutherford left his breakfast in the dirt, and swore off chicken indefinitely.

# CHAPTER 7

The thick canopy of trees overhead erased any underfoot shadow the noonday sun would have drawn from the troop of sharpshooters, and it gave them a thin sense of security like the hook on an outhouse door. The anxiety that floated along with them slowed down time and made their hour long hustle around the battle field feel more like a fifty mile death march. To them every tree hid a short fused Confederate and each hollow an entire regiment, waiting just for them, rifles cocked and aimed, trigger fingers itching. All the while as they leaped through the woods, the beast of war snarled louder and closer, booming cannons its breathe, pops of the rifles were the sound of great teeth slamming shut on some poor soul.

Small whispered banter kept them moving, mindlessly giving thanks to the mild weather and the thinness of the autumnal undergrowth. Hiram began to fall back to the rear of the procession, partially to avoid the small talk he always failed at, mostly so as to be one of the last targets in the event of an ambush. The madmen and future suicides like Father Death and Hobb lead the way, still creeping and dodging for cover, like the rest of the men; but not as quietly, with close focused eyes hoping to find their death close at hand rather than far afield. Looking for the one last blaze of glory that might at least pay back half of their unspoken sins.

Brecht pretended to get caught up in a dry, nettle rich copse, but he was really just dawdling until Hiram pulled up the rear. Hiram saw Brecht's face twist up as he passed. The young one easily tore from the briers and caught up with him.

"Sure are hanging back. Feeling a little yellow?"

"Not at all, I've this trick knee acting up." Hiram made a show of heroic limping.

"Never seen you stumble along like that."

"She only acts up when idiots ask damn-fool questions."

Brecht paced along for a dozen numb steps until the insult landed. He sped up and trudged at pace, bumping shoulder to shoulder with Hiram, pressing him into the path of branches and bushes.

"See here, I know what you've been up to, you blackguard. I've seen you skulking around the officer's tents."

"I'm just trying to stay out of the reach of your stink, friend."

It was two paces until that breached Brecht's skull. When it did he frowned and rammed a well-placed elbow into Hiram's side.

"You cocky son-of-a-bitch. No jokes. I know what you are. Now, listen here. I'm, about as bully for this war as a sow is for the slaughter house, but if I find out you've been spying, I'll open you up myself." He chuckled and leaped over a log.

"I'll wait till you're asleep, I've got a knife so sharp you won't even wake up when I do it."

Hiram feigned a stumble and knocked Brecht into a gnarly tree. The rest of the troop continued unknowing while Hiram pinned the smaller soldier with a forearm over his windpipe. Hiram growled.

"You'd do better to keep your nose clean and worry about the rebels over that next hill." He pressed harder, making Brecht gag.

Hiram released and jogged off to catch up with the rest of the men.

Brecht coughed and spat. His eyes seemed to pinch closer together as he scowled after Hiram, he bared his sharp cracked teeth. The hatred in his eyes was heavy and grey, hot like molten lead.

"Dirty, yellow, spy." He spat, as he ran to catch up.

The battle was close, they slowed down and proceeded, hunched low, the only sound they made was the click-snap of the men checking their rifles and the broken hiss that the mouth makes when whispering prayers. When they caught sight of the break in the trees the captain motioned for them to take a knee.

When he spoke none of the men looked at him. They busied themselves with bootlaces and rifles. Hobb had stuck a dry plug of tobacco in his lip and kept smacking, trying to drum up enough saliva to get it moist. Father Death took the tattered little map he'd been using to guide them and spread it out on the leaves.

"If the scout was correct, our target should be six hundred yards out. We're up on a hill, have the high ground." His finger traced the snaking line of the valley that made up the battlefield. "Wrathbone ordered a full charge-"

He paused and cleared his throat as though mentioning the order had left something foul in him.

"We're going to have troops on the ground damn near everywhere, just focus here, to the east. Should be three or four big guns, probably the ones they've been using to chuck those quartermaster hunters at us."

He took out a dented steel pocket watch and pried open its cover with a dirty thumbnail.

"We have ten minutes. We take out those guns, or at least keep them busy enough, then there's a chance our boys can swing around and flank the enemy." He folded the map up and shoved it back into a pocket. "If we get spotted and have to regroup, break west; at least we can pull the focus of their fire off our men on the field." He pulled his rifle from his shoulder and the rest followed suit.

"As always, if any of you fine men decide it prudent to go off on your own hook, you will soon find it difficult to run with a pair of slugs in your legs."

The captain allowed his rare smile to flash below the mustache and in a blink it was gone. The younger men shivered, remembering the pie-eater the captain had crippled three missions ago. The bumpkin had only fled twenty feet before he fell with a bullet in his knee.

"Stay low, pick your shots. Aim small, miss small..." He waved his hand, bored. "Care to favor us with a prayer, Hobb?"

Hobb had finally gotten the tobacco juicy. He spat a brown gout.

"Nope."

"Amen. Let's move up."

They inched their way to the ridge, squinting in the light of the thinning canopy. The crest of the ridge was high enough that when they crawled up to it nothing could be seen beyond it but the dirty sky.

The war sounds were strong, but muted by the dense rise of dirt. As they drew closer, nearly peeking over the edge, Hiram had the feeling of a child both excited and afraid to look into a forbidden box. Father Death motioned for them to halt and snapped out his field glass. His knees popped as he bent even further down and edged the last few yards to the tree line.

"Let's see how well that scout did his job."

He popped his head up into exposure and efficiently scanned all before him with the tarnished glass. The men were all silent watching him, breathing in unison, picking nervously at scabs on their faces, snags in their uniforms. The captain dropped down and snapped the glass shut. His face was blank, but somehow terrifying, like peering into a dark and empty room.

"We've been had, they know we're-"

They heard the roar of the cannonball ripping through the air before the top of the hill exploded into a deadly cloud of dirt and shrapnel. The captain was thrown forward and slammed into Hobb, who rolled him off immediately into Brecht's lap. Brecht screamed while the captain clawed the dirt in agony. His back was still smoking around the dozen holes that had been punched through him. His cap was nowhere to be seen; the first time the men had seen him without it.

Brecht crawled out from beneath the silently writhing man and continued to crab-walk backward, pale faced, until a tree stopped him.

Hiram thought he could hear a church bell ringing not far off, but it wasn't a series of sounds, just one long clang that spun in his head. Hobb crawled to the captain and flipped him over. He lifted the bloody man by the lapels and shouted something at him that Hiram couldn't make out, everything sounded like a rushing river.

He heard the second shell, though; it sounded like a great sheet of paper as wide as the sky being ripped in half. It cruised over the crest of the hill and pulverized the base of an ancient oak that stood nearby. Splinters exploded from it like a shotgun blast and Hiram could see from a dizzy spin of his head that every man but Brecht had been struck by them.

One man rolled on the ground, his mouth open wide in a howl that Hiram couldn't hear over the rapids in his ears. The man's face was spangled with splinters of wood like a witch's pin-cushion; his eyes had swollen instantly shut. Hobb had taken a gnarly shard to his thigh, but he ignored it as he hollered at Father Death.

Hiram didn't hear the third blast; he only saw dirt rain down from above as one of the greenhorns jumped to his feet. The new recruit took three shuddering steps and fell face down into the red clay, his neck artery open wide like a second mouth pumping nauseously. Hiram tried to stand and run, but the world pitched up toward him and he landed right back on his knees.

There was something wrong with him. His neck felt like there were bugs inside of it, dancing in the meat to the beat of his heart. He pawed at the maddening itch with numb fingers as the water started to drain from his ears. He preferred the mute of that river. Everyone was screaming or crying.

He found the splinter sticking next to his windpipe. Yanking it out felt like a match being struck inside of him.

The burning pop of pain gave him focus and half of the dizziness washed away with the cold sweat that bloomed on his skin. Hobb was shaking the lifeless body of Father Death, shouting all around him at the chaos of soldiers.

"Captain says we got to regroup over West and try a shot from there. *Listen* to me, varmints! Wast! Let's go!"

Hobb set off at a quick limp, the shard of tree still stuck in place. None of the men followed him. Hiram swung his rifle around to ready and began a careful jog back the way they had come. Brecht was still lying with his back to the tree. It looked like the tree had protected him. He was unscathed but his face was pale and there was an idiot madness in his eyes that belonged in an asylum. He shouted after Hiram as he passed.

"I knew it was you! You no good, yellow, son-of-a-*whore*. Get back here!"

Hiram ignored him and picked up the pace, trying to leave the noise of war behind him. But he couldn't, it was all around him now, distant but ever present. Just through the trees, over the hills, in the sky and the earth and in his head. Men were dying and there was no way he could help and nothing he could do to get away. He tugged his bandanna higher on his neck to cover the wound. There wasn't much blood; it had driven through a rare bit of flesh un-knotted by blood vessels, the only lucky thing to happen to him for weeks.

He ran; hopping stumps, thrashing branches aside as they reached for him, every twig hungry and snagging. He could still feel the splinter that had been in his neck and it was driving him mad, every three steps he would swat at the phantom itch and curse.

His eyes still saw, just as his ears still heard, but every sense was muffled in goose feathers.

He knew he ran past trees and mud and rocks, but they all streamed past him like he was running through an oil painter's still wet canvas. The rustle of leaves scraping his face, brushing his shoulders, crunching underfoot. They too turned liquid in his ear until all he could hear were a hundred rowdy children wrestling in a titanic pile of dry leaves

His mind grabbed this fancy as he ran; he started to flesh out the children, who they were, how they fought. He watched the children in the theater of his mind while the trees and mud smeared by, painting the children all sorts of colors that didn't belong on them. The pile of leaves heaved with each sharp lungful of air he wretched in, like there was something huge and hideous slumbering within it.

"Hiram!" One of the children screamed, but it wasn't a child's voice; it was that of a madman.

Hiram snapped from the vision and glanced over his shoulder. Brecht was charging after him, hat off and pistol out.

*"You. Are. Dead!"*

The words pumped from the man's straining lungs and the gun popped. Hiram flinched and ducked, barely leaping over a log in his path. The bullet buzzed through the leaves and branches where his head had only just been.

*"Brecht! It wasn't-"* Hiram shouted back, but another shot cracking from behind made him take evasive action, dodging off the path where there was more cover. He threaded back and forth between the trees like the forest was a great green needlepoint frame. Brecht was still not far behind, screaming with every breath.

Hiram pounded hard, gaining as much ground as his heavy legs would let him, pulling his revolver and thumbing back the hammer. He burst into a clearing and slid to a stop, spinning on his heels and taking aim at the brush where Brecht was about to...

There he was. Brecht's head sitting perfectly above Hiram's sight. Brecht's eyes widened from the menacing wince once he saw the big bore pistol waiting to remove his face. His own gun swung up to Hiram, they were only ten feet apart. Both men could see down the endless tunnels of the barrel's facing them, mine-shafts leading down into places where men could never return. The precipitous feeling of standing close to the edge of a canyon while the animal of the body recoils, howling in alarm that death is close.

Both men fired.

# CHAPTER 8

Narcisse held his lips tight and his eyes forward as he was pulled through the Union camp. He allowed himself to be moved, but did not make it easy for the soldiers that flanked him on either side.

"Made quite a name for yourself, huh?" Said Rutherford. He was a head shorter then Narcisse, but acted like he towered over the black man.

"I saw that chicken you brought back, still got me shook up."

The other soldier whinnied and spat.

"It was a trick, it was nothing." Narcisse slowed just enough to make them stumble.

"Pick up the pace. Don't want to have to keep a rifle at your back." They jerked him forward, pushing him closer to the general's tent. Narcisse's lips twitched in silent prayer:

*These that not mine know no protection-*
*These that not mine know my wrath-*
*So it is- So it be.*

The constant crackle of rifle fire crawled over the hill that protected the camp. At the top, a skeleton crew of artillery men struggled to keep the big guns fed. The cannons were firing at half the rate they had been earlier when the offensive had begun. The barrel of one of the cannons had been blasted from its mount by a direct hit; it lay in the path, dug down into the clay.

The pack mule it had taken with it lay about in gory shambles, hacked to bits by the camp's cooks. Rutherford shook his head and continued.

"Wasn't any trick like I've ever seen, that sucker had its neck snapped and feathers off. I've been to three circuses and a magic show and never seen anything like that, Hoodoo man."

"It's not Hoodoo, mon ami." Narcisse tried to lock the soldier's eye, but his cornflower blue gaze never wandered from the path. They approached a large tent with a star painted on it.

"Well, that's just grand-" The soldier moved to pull the heavy oilcloth flap to the side but stopped when a booming voice erupted screaming from within, so much so that the walls of the tent seemed to billow outward.

"You can call it whatever you want, it's got General Wrathbone interested in you."

The flap burst open and a young enlisted man tripped through, his face moist with silent tears.

"You lucky buck, you've got the general on a good day." Rutherford sneered.

Narcisse bared his uncanny teeth at the soldier, but was once again ignored. His escorts took him by his ropey arms and pulled him along into the tent.

"Mind your manners." The other soldier said, and spat a gout of brown phlegm before they passed through.

The tent was murky like the bijou inside. One of the two lamps that lit it had a shaggy untrimmed wick that sputtered and made the shadows in the hollows of every man's face twitch left and right like they were glancing cautiously. Cigar smoke was thick and eye-watering. There was a whiskey smell heavy enough to bead up on their skin.

The general sat slumped back in his chair; his face was obscured by his hand, fingers pinching the bridge of his nose. A cigar burned in a brass ashtray with a dozen of its fallen brothers. There were two amber bottles on the desk, one of them empty the other well on its way.

He blindly felt in the direction of his tin cup.

"Leave us." The general muttered, his voice rough from smoke.

The soldiers didn't seem to like the idea, looking at each other they shuffled their boots indecisively.

"Go!"

They shoved Narcisse closer and turned to leave. The blonde one hissed;

"You try any tricks and we will be in here at the drop of a hat."

Once they were alone, the General sat up in his chair. His eyes were a bit too small for his face and red with drink.

"Mr. Narcisse, I presume."

"You is co-rect, massah, but I don't know you name." He flashed his oversized smile that seemed to leap off of his face.

"And that is how it shall remain." The general laughed and puffed on the cigar stub until it glowed back to life. "I know better than to tell you my Christian name."

Narcisse's smile came down like a theater curtain.

"I hardly think dat is co-jial, but if gen-ral is scared..."

"Enough!" He stood up, slammed a big bore Navy revolver on the desk and leaned over it. He continued in a whisper.

"You listen to me you tricky son of a bitch, you are going to take a seat and listen to what I have to say-"

He picked up a legal document from his desk that made Narcisse's eyes go wide for a moment.

"And when I'm done you will answer me yes or no. If that answer is no, your Freeman Papers are going to light my next cigar." His face looked hot and veins stood out on his fevered forehead.

"If you do anything else I'm going to blow the sin right out of you." He brought up his cuff to dab at his brow.

Narcisse balked, if only for a moment.

"As you say, I do, massah." Narcisse sat in the only chair.

"I'm not any man's master." He sat and took a long sip from the tin cup. The revolver was still pointed at Narcisse.

"You do act like it, Gen'ral."

The hammer clicked back in the revolver and the general's eyes glowed up from beneath his heavy brow.

Narcisse smiled wider than before.

"I listnin'."

"You may or may not know that we are taking a beating out there. I just received word that three quarters of our men have fallen, and the remaining should be arriving back here at camp within the hour. I have more dead men under my command than live ones."

He cleared his throat and topped off his cup.

"We are in no state to fight should the enemy follow the retreating soldiers. Even if we are lucky enough to have a quiet night we do not have the supplies to last more than three days. Even if we could hold our line they could easily starve us out." He took a deep draw of the cigar and painted the room with it. "We haven't heard from our reinforcements in a week."

"Aw, it look like all is lost, Gen'ral." Narcisse spoke as if to an infant. The smile never left his face.

"This is why I called for you. Your reputation precedes you. Your ways with, -with the dead."

"But I just a travellin' salesman, sellin' dese fine charms and doodads-" He was cut off by the tin cup flying at his head. He dodged but his face was still splashed with liquor.

"I will remind you of my warning!" Roared the general, revolver shaking in his hand. "Speak plainly to me."

Narcisse only nodded slowly, smiling.

"I've heard about the work you lay long before we caught you. All the runaways know your name and only speak it in hushed tones. They say you are powerful in the spirit world." He whispered.

"Some people say that."

The general took a swig directly from the bottle.

"I've prayed to the lord every night since I put on my uniform, and I've not *once* stopped talking to him since I was put in command of these men."

His eyes screwed up and he spoke through gritted teeth like someone was twisting his arm.

"And no matter how much I pray and *beg*, things just keep getting worse. Two thousand of my men have been slaughtered. I won't see a thousand more die because god didn't hear their cries..." His voice was wavering. He took another drink.

"So, I begin thinking, maybe I'm praying to the wrong god? Maybe mine has given up on us?" He put the revolver down and rubbed his face with his hands.

"I can help, monsieur."

The general looked up at him with moist eyes. "Do I have your word?"

"Oh, of course." Smile unchanging.

"What, what do you need from me?"

"Cigars, whiskey, and a top hat."

"I can get you the first two, haven't seen a top hat since I left Illinois.

* * *

All eyes were on Narcisse as he exited the general's tent with a front pocket full of slim cigars and a corked bottle of whiskey under his arm. Rutherford dashed into his path and leveled his rifle at Narcisse's face.

"What did you do to the General, Hoodoo Man?"

Narcisse held out a note that was clearly in the general's shaky hand. It ordered any enlisted man to assist Narcisse in any way possible.

The soldier squinted at the note and shook his head.

"Not sure what you did, but don't think this note will let you get away with bloody murder."

"I did no-thing. Your master beg me an' mine for help." He sauntered forward until the soldier's rifle was resting cool and oily on the crease of his forehead.

"I don't know about that." Rutherford squeaked.

"You're right, you don't know 'bout dat."

They stood eye to eye for a dozen moments. The stare-down was broken when a shell hit the ridge, sending the jumpier men running for cover. Dirt rained down over the camp.

"If Wrathbone orders-"

"He do."

That terrible smile.

"Mmph," The soldier scratched under his cap. "The second you try anything-"

"Then you shoot me at the drop of a hat." Narcisse's smile was like a razor.

The soldier was still scratching his head. "None of this can be Christian."

"How many men you killed, Rutherford?"

The soldier froze, nodded slowly and motioned for Narcisse to lead the way.

Narcisse shuffled his feet, making his heavy manacles clink.

"But first, how 'bout you just take these off?"

\* \* \*

"Happy now, you goddamned heathen? We got you a chicken and candles and who knows what." Rutherford had borne the same confused expression the whole afternoon he had spent gathering supplies with Narcisse.

"I need drummers." said Narcisse, striding to the tent that had been emptied for his purposes.

"You think we have a damned pennywhistle between us just now? We haven't had a use for a band since-"

"You left Illinois." Narcisse said it like 'Illi-nwah'.

"Christ sakes, stop that."

"I need drummers for... control."

"I could hum the Battle Hymn for you if you please, but by my word there isn't a drum for five miles."

"This will be difficult."

"So was wrestling that hen from the cooks. You'd better get started conjuring or whatever the blazes you have planned." Rutherford dropped the supplies in front of the vacant tent.

"I don't want anything to do with it." He tilted his hat down over his eyes; he noticed it was easier to resist the Hoodoo-man when his eyes were covered.

"Mark my words, you try to sneak out of that tent you won't make it ten paces."

Narcisse only snatched up the supplies and left the soldier with a grin that seemed to hang in the air after he was gone.

Rutherford shook his head and began creeping around the tent, muttering under his breath;

"I *know* you're just a chiseler, a no good liar..."

\* \* \*

Narcisse was sweating, but not from the stifling heat of the candle spangled tent. He had been afraid a number of times while he was learning The Mystery of Voodoo, but he had never been truly terrified.

Once the tent flap dropped and he was all alone, the smile ran from his face and his mouth tensed into an O. The sweat started rolling down.

He was about to invoke Baron Samedi, the trickiest of all the Loa spirits. He didn't have any protection at all. No drummers to distract, no singers to chant and contain the spirit. All he had were some cut-rate offerings and his own body. He hoped that it would be enough, not for the success of the white man's army, but for the protection of his mind, body, and soul.

His hand trembled as he poured the whiskey and it took four matches to get the cigar lit, his panting breath repeatedly extinguished them. He was mentally calling out to his ancestors for protection, though he knew in his heart that he had crossed them too many times to expect any kind of mercy from them. He was a condemned man, and the altar was his gallows.

The candles were lit and everything was in place. He drew the dagger and anointed it as he had so many times before. His chant was the deepest and most powerful he had ever pulled from himself.

The sack by his side stirred. Chickens always sleep when it is dark, no matter where they are. Something was wrong if it was waking up. Narcisse chanted louder, speeding up, hurrying to the climax. He squeezed his eyes shut to keep the stinging sweat out and reds and yellows bloomed on the insides of his lids.

It grew cold in the tent, far colder than it was outside. He could not tell if the roaring in his head was from the blood charging through his ears, or if it was the howling of wounded soldiers being dragged back from the killing fields.

He reached the final line of the ceremony and bellowed it over and over, his elbows tight to his side, convulsing and bowing. He tore the bag open and yanked the fluttering hen from within. He snapped his eyes open so he could see where to properly open the chicken up. Freezing, he stared at the dark corner of the tent. His mouth was slack and the only thing to be heard was Narcisse's labored breathing. Even the hen was silent.

"Go on 'head, boy. *Blood deh best paht.*"

Baron Samedi was in the room. It smelled like a funeral home and nickel cologne.

Narcisse couldn't stop shaking. The trembling knife cast an oval of light that danced over the spirit, who grinned as though tickled by a lover. He stepped closer to Narcisse. His garish top hat was nearly as dusty as his long coat. He was skeletal thin with ashy grey skin and his face nothing but a bobbing skull above a rumpled collar. The Baron's eyes were empty and black, like the pupils were stretched so wide they could watch everything in the world. He laughed and it hit Narcisse as though he were standing near a kettle drum.

"Kill dat chicken, I hunger." Even his tongue was bone. It rattled like a snake tail charm.

Narcisse brought up the dagger and with one jerking cluck the chicken spilled its life into the tin bowl with pulsing gouts. Narcisse could not blink. He had summoned and been mounted by myriads of the Loa, but he had never seen them with his eyes like this.

It seemed like the skeletal Loa never stopped laughing. It responded as if it had read the bokor's mind.

"There many, many, dead man tonight. I came quick to dig graves for they souls." Bare grinning teeth snapped together three times, clacking like claves. "But you, mon ami, call me up with dis fine cigar and middlin' whiskey-"

The Loa's bony fingers reached out and caught the stream of blood. They caught every drop, even sucking up what had spilled on the floor. In a moment the spirit was vibrating with life and those grinning teeth were in Narcisse's face.

He dropped the carcass and drew back in terror.

"You so 'fraid, but you deh man dat call me!" Baron Samedi roared.

"I can tell dis will be enta-tainin', much more den diggin' graves, mon ami." He held out his hand and the chicken's body floated up to meet it. A violet aura washed out from the Loa's fingertips and the body came to life, its severed neck making the head hang askew, cocked like it was asking an endless question. It began to croak 'Camptown Ladies'.

Narcisse felt a terrible numbness all over him, like the dreams he'd had where he was paralyzed and attacked by demons. He couldn't even speak. It felt like his soul was sinking down into the cold deep clay of his body. His eyes were becoming tunnels, ribbed caves that lost sight of living color as he sank.

"Ha! I know what you want, but you must ask me, oui? Down on dem knees!"

As Narcisse sank deeper he felt the cold of the grave in his bones, and the fleeting scent of humanity, the kind a loved one smells when hovering over the newly dead. He tried to speak, to say anything, but his jaw was locked.

"Ah-hah! Mon ami, you haven't answered. I just do what I want, then. Have a little fun."

Narcisse tried to say no, to stop the spirit, but he was too far down the well.

* * *

A scream ripped through the whole camp that set all the animals skittish. Outside the tent, Rutherford jumped and steadied his rifle.

"What in the goddamn hell-" He said.

Narcisse slid sideways through the flap, his head aslant, hands bloody. He was slapping the gory blade of the dagger against his thigh. Rutherford leveled the rifle at him.

"Stop right there! Drop that knife! What was all that yelling?"

His smile had changed in a way turned Rutherford's stomach. Narcisse tucked the knife into the back of his pants and held out his hands, but continued to creep up on the soldier.

"Stay where you are!" Rutherford was trembling. There was something wrong in the air. Narcisse continued on his path, his teeth looking too big for his head.

"I need your hat, mon ami." He drew closer.

"This will be the last time I tell you!" Rutherford pulled the hammer back on his rifle.

Narcisse threw his hands in the air and spun flamboyantly. By the time Rutherford fired, Narcisse had smacked the barrel to the side and his other hand had swung around. The dagger whistled through the soldier's neck.

Rutherford stood dumb for a moment, the blood rolled down his neck like a red carpet. Narcisse plucked the cap off of his head.

"I get dis back to you tomorrow." He looked the hat over and placed it on his head. "Don't like it, but it will do."

The soldier fell to his knees then to his side. The whites of his eyes rolled up to Narcisse.

"It time for Baron Samedi to lay down some work." He knelt by a dying cook-fire, took up a palm full of ashes and rubbed them over his face.

"Haven't had fun like dis in a coon's age." He blacked out circles around his eyes with a stick of charred wood. He puffed the cigar he held in his teeth back to life and began to saunter in the direction of the general's tent.

\* \* \*

The amber bottle was empty when the ashy man waved himself past the guards and let himself into the general's quarters. The revolver was still on the desk, but the barrel was pointing at Wrathbone now.

The general was slouched back in his chair, eyes wide, wider still when Baron Samedi walked in. Each breath sounded like an effort.

"Good evenin', Rat-bone. You deh one asked Narcisse for the miracle?"

"What-" The general pushed himself into a slightly more upright position. "What the hell are you talking about? If you're trying to make a fool of me I'll have you-"

Baron Samedi exhaled a cloud of smoke that seemed too thick for the slim cigar to produce and snaked his crooked fingers through it in a gesture. The general's cup lifted from the table and flew swiftly into the Baron's hand, not spilling a drop. He tossed it back and swallowed. A scream curdled its way from the medic's tent.

"I'm Baron Samedi, and you'll call me dis. There's no Narcisse no more."

The general's mouth moved like he wanted to talk, but no sound came out. The Baron gave a small but extravagant bow.

"I'm at you service, but you-" He snapped his fingers. "You in my debt, mon ami. If I get all dose southern boys dead for you-" He waved a finger at the ceiling and flashed the whites of his eyes as well as his teeth, "I'm going to need some kine' a payment."

The general's wrinkled skin squinted up around his little eyes.

"Name your price, spirit." He reached for a cup that was no longer there and exhaled through his nose.

The red glow of the cigar lit up the high hard ridges of the Baron's face as he puffed. The long thin hands came up and lay athwart his chest.

"Ah, you see, Gen-ral, I'm deh Loa of deh dead. It my job to dig deh grave of souls dat get free from deh body."

His arms went wide and he took a step closer. "Dis hard work, you know. An' men like you make a terrible lot of it." He put his hands down on the table and began stroking the revolver that lay there.

"My payment would be dat I don't hav'ta dig dem graves, give me a little vacation, huh? They already dead, what've you got to lose?"

"I- don't rightly know." There were tears in the general's eyes. He was buttoning and unbuttoning the collar of his shirt.

"Come now, gen-ral," The Baron's eyes seemed to sink away, turning into black little pits. "How many more of your boys need to die when dem rebels start shootin' again?"

The general couldn't seem to blink any longer. The corners of his eyes were moist. The Baron reached out his hand to him.

"I can help?" The cigar had attached itself to the corner of his cracked, ashy lips. "Oui?"

The general slowly reached out and shook the hand. The color had dropped from his face.

"Do what you must, spirit. I fear I have just lost my soul."

"Don' worry, mon ami." The Baron snuffed out the cigar underfoot and put a fresh one in its place. "It already been spoken for."

# CHAPTER 9

Hiram's mind had been a maelstrom throughout the run back to camp. The shell blast had seemingly knocked something loose in his mind that hadn't yet fallen back into place. There were a number of voices echoing within, each shouting louder than the other, fighting for control. In that last cold-sweat moment when Brecht charged out of the woods, two of the voices had rung clear and wrestled at Hiram's gun. One of them screamed, *'Kill him, protect yourself.',* while the other pleaded with him to keep running.

At the final possible second Hiram had found a neutral place, quieting the two voices but pleasing neither. He had shifted his aim and shot Brecht in the shoulder, the close range of the blast throwing the screaming soldier's aim askew and dropping him whimpering but alive into the leaves.

He had survived, but none of the voices thought he had done the right thing. Hiram rarely felt vindicated in any of his decisions. Everything came at a cost. Once he was clear of the battle he decided to return to camp for one last attempt at stealing the plans. Without them he was a dead man, whether he made it out of the battle or not.

The closer he got to the border of the camp, the sicker he felt. Something was very wrong. There were no men on patrol as far as he could see and a strange silence had settled over the area, like the spirits of the men had sunk with the sun. He had heard that the general ordered a forward push, but even one as mad as Wrathbone couldn't order every living man onto the battlefield.

Part of him felt he should explore further, but he knew that if he had any chance of stealing the plans, now was the time.

He walked to the rear of the camp as he had often done before. The silence was driving him mad. Only the far off echoes of cannons roaring made it that far back from the battlefield. Sounds usually hidden by the constant murmur of men and clink of gear rose eerily to the forefront.

A cool wood-smoke wind blew in from the east, whistling through the threadbare canvas of hundreds of tents, their untied flaps waving and slapping at Hiram as he slunk past. It sounded like the whole camp was moaning.

On his way to the general's tent he stopped at his own. He had thought the camp had been hastily evacuated, all of his things swept up in a tide of fleeing men; but everything was just as he left it. His shotgun was tucked under his bedroll, right next to his repeater. His heavy rucksack was packed and ready to go, as he always kept it, knowing that someday he would have to make a hasty exit.

He thought for one last moment before leaving, and tossed through his bunkmate's things, assuming whatever happened to the squirrely little man, that he wouldn't need them anymore. He turned up an ammo box with firing caps and a hunk of pemmican, all wrapped up in an indigo bandanna. Stuffing these into his pack, and turning to go, he stopped short of pulling back the tent flap. There was movement outside.

The sound of a great procession. Dozens of boots struggling and scuffing against a ponderous weight. Hiram peered cautiously through an unpatched hole in the tent. He saw pass dozens of straining legs, followed by the wheels of horse carts, over-laden with branches and cords of wood.

They were soldiers of the Union, which brought a sliver of relief to Hiram, but he couldn't imagine why they would be hauling so much wood to the front of the camp. It didn't make sense. Relief gave way to fear.

They were eerily silent in their labor, with none of the grunts and curses that usually accompany men hard at work.

It was almost as though they were of one mind.

Something clicked in Hiram's mind. The wood-smoke smell on the wind. They were building a fire. A big one. It wasn't even dark yet. A great blaze built before sundown was a sinister thing.

He listened and waited for the tramp of feet and the creak of the axles to fade before he left the tent. He returned to his hasty creep toward the rear of the camp. He didn't have the time to ponder what strange fate had befallen the soldiers, he kept moving.

He dodged two more strange parades of puppet soldiers, laden with gear of all sorts, their faces dumb and pale as unpainted wax statues. It was like a spigot had been opened in their bellies that drained the humanity from them. He was thankful that they weren't on the hunt; for if they were half as staunch in battle as they were at hauling he would be a goner before the sun set.

If anything, he was too cautious. By the time he had made it back to the command tent the sun had sunk behind the far off crest of the protecting ridge, and the sounds of war had ceased completely.

The silence of the camp was twice as maddening as the roar of constant battle. He imagined a legion of waiting ears, listening to every crunch of his heavy boots, each clink of gear in his overfull pack; but he made it to his goal unmolested.

It was liberating to stride to the front of the General's tent, to not creep behind it in the fetid alley. Hiram pondered as he passed into the still, silent tent, that one simply had to wait for the right moment to make a move, and often the hard work would be done for you.

He allowed a smile to crease his lips as he approached the desk. There they were. The plans, maps, documents, and orders lay naked on the desk, blowing slightly in the draft beneath the leaden weights that held them down.

He felt anxious things crawling behind his belly button. He walked silently; though he was sure no one was around, his eyes darting back over his shoulder with every step.

Once he reached the desk, all caution flew from him and he snatched at the papers like a starving dog would descend upon table scraps. The weights slid from the maps and clattered down to the wood, sounding like dice on a backgammon board.

Hiram tried to carefully fold the expanses of paper, but every moment he spent at the task multiplied his panic, until he was nearly stuffing them into his rucksack. His shaking hands knocked over an empty bottle which tipped with a thunk and rolled to the edge of the desk.

Hiram's reflexes stole his arm and it bolted out, map in hand, and he succeeded only in knocking the bottle into a spin that brought it closer and closer to the edge until, with one slow indecise rotation, it plummeted and smashed against the rocky dirt below.

The jolt of the crash made Hiram straighten in alarm, but after a moment of silence he regained his nerve and set to folding the creasy, finger stained map. It sounded like children, far off, playing in leaves.

"I'll kill myself before I let you take me."

Hiram froze.

The wasted visage of General Wrathbone was suddenly before him. He popped up from behind the desk in a flash and stood with one pistol at his temple and another pointed at Hiram. Hiram didn't drop the map in his hands; he hugged it to his chest.

"Get back." The General grunted, pulling himself shakily to his feet. There wasn't an inch of him that wasn't rumpled. It looked like he had been sleeping behind the desk. The sight of the revolver never left Hiram, who stopped breathing while his mind spun, looking for some exit.

"You're not one of them." The General got out with some difficulty.

"No, no, sir!" Hiram thought quickly. "I thought the entire camp was, ehm, afflicted, so when I returned from my mission, I decided to protect your documents, so as they wouldn't fall into enemy hands."

The General laughed. It sounded like something being dragged out of a hole.

"And, who's the enemy?"

Hiram knew the question was rhetorical, but he answered anyway.

"The rebels, sir. It looks like they've cleared out the camp."

"You missed all of it, didn't you?" The General put down the pistol that had been pointing at his head and ran his fingers through his untrimmed hair.

"It would appear I did, sir. What happened?"

The General sat heavily in his chair and exhaled more air than it seemed he could hold.

"Mistakes were made." His free hand rummaged through the litter on the desk, shaking bottle after bottle until he found one that wasn't empty. "Too drunk to explain." He finished the bottle and let out a phlegmy cough. "The men you see in the camp aren't men anymore."

"All of them are afflicted like that, sir?"

"You shouldn't call your hangman 'Sir'."

The gun wavered in Wrathbone's hand.

His head sunk down slowly like a ponderous weight descending below water. His free hand caught it before it hit the table. The general spoke again.

"I'm- Oh. I'm terribly dizzy right now. You need to go." He coughed so long and hard, Hiram feared the General might wretch.

"Take the papers. I don't think it matters anymore."

The general placed the revolver that had been trained on Hiram down on the desk next to its sister.

"I don't care who you really are, or what you plan to do with those papers, just get out of here as fast as you can. Don't let the ashen man see you. Don't let anyone see you."

His hand crawled blindly over the desk until it found the revolver. His gnawed finger began to trace each well forged contour, the crescent of the small of a lover's back, the curve of a hip.

"Tell them it was all Wrathbone's fault, that- that the shame could be placed on no else."

Hiram's face burned from keeping the emotion away from it.

He crumpled the last of the documents into his rucksack.

"You won't be forgotten, sir."

"Dear god, I pray that I am." Wrathbone picked up the pistol, every atom of him shaking, nothing but a skeleton dressed in the ill-fitting skin of a man.

"Leave me, so I can die in peace." He massaged the barrel of the revolver over his scalp. His face bore the strangest smile Hiram had ever seen. The general whispered so it barely crossed the desk.

"Go. Go. Go..."

Hiram shouldered his pack and left without a salute.

Wrathbone forced his eyes open once more. He slapped the cylinder of the Navy into a spin. He brought the muzzle into his mouth. It brought back memories from his childhood, hiding pennies under his tongue so his poor mother wouldn't take them from him. He had done her wrong. He had done everyone wrong.

"Please. Lord. Hell can't be any worse than this."

Then, the loudest sound in the world.

# CHAPTER 10

Narcisse was cold. He still felt his body in an abstract, burning way; the way that one can feel smothering in a dream. He was deep in a well within himself, watching his body do things he did not order, through eyes he could not close. Narcisse had never once wished for death, but this cold, sick half-life he had plunged into was making him ponder it.

He saw the bonfire. He felt the static crackle in the air, the energy coming from his own body. The still eyes of the enraptured soldiers encircling him. Saw the sacrifice of the prisoner, and felt the life flow into him. All the energy twisting and curling into one focused point of red heat, pressing and squeezing until it was a pinprick as hot as the blinding white heart of a blacksmith's forge. It was painful to hold within him, but he had no choice. Like a flaming bullet that stayed vibrating within his ribs.

He felt something open in him that hadn't been there a second before. So much flowed through the hole that he wanted to scream, but the baron was in full control and the only thing to leave his mouth was mad laughter. Narcisse couldn't see the maelstrom of energy gathering in him, but he imagined what it looked like. The pinprick of light turning cold and opening up like a gate before a battering ram. A rushing stampede bursting through him, coming from somewhere frigid and black.

Narcisse didn't know what was silently thundering through him as the Baron lifted the limp prisoner and threw him onto the bonfire, but it felt like something sterile, a white light burning cold and stripped of all colors, shades, and hues. He wanted the feeling to stop more than anything he had ever wanted in his life.

He felt the energy radiate in all directions, saw the charred corpse stand when the Baron beckoned it to do so. He saw the pink mist collect, seemingly from nowhere. The Baron saw the lone man in the watchtower and sent the corpse after him when he ran.

# CHAPTER 11

Only a few hours before the ashen man had been in shackles. Now he stood in a clearing, directing the building of a great bonfire. Baron Samedi rarely stopped laughing and never ceased smiling. His face had become so terrible to behold that even the most hardened veterans averted their gaze when he passed. There was an unclean smell on the air and the setting sun drew a red brush over the whole camp. The men seemed to change as it grew darker.

At first it had required pistol shots to get the soldiers to follow the orders of the Baron. Now they heeded him without a word of protest, their eyes on the ground ahead of them, steps slow and heavy with some invisible burden.

Nearly the whole camp acted this way, save for the Irish guard up in the watch tower and the general, who leaned askew against the flagpole giving off a flammable odor. He tried to get the attention of passing soldiers, but succeeded in getting only slow glances from their lazy eyes. By the time the sun had set, he had given up.

The guard began shouting from the watch tower as soon as match was touched to oil and the bonfire roared to life. The only person in the camp that noticed the blustering Irishman was the Baron, who only pointed and laughed at him. The scout ceased the shouting and boiled down to pacing a little circle in the hastily built tower.

As the fire grew, so did the shuffling circle of soldiers around it, seemingly without directions from Baron Samedi.

The general swayed against the flag pole, an empty flask at his feet. Despite the shivers that washed over his body, his fingers moved slowly and precisely over the pistol as he checked the actions, over and over.

A low hum, almost a chant, rose up from the mass of soldiers. Baron Samedi stood in the center of the circle, arms upraised with the wicked dagger in one hand. He was so close to the fire one could see the steam rising from his skin.

The guard stopped his pacing upon hearing the chant. He grabbed his rifle and pack and scampered down the ladder. He saw the general's long shadow wavering in the fire light and ran to him.

"General, sir, what kind of devilry is goin' on? Why'd you stand by and watch this happen?"

The general didn't look up from the revolver. "I ordered this, Private Declan."

Declan looked at the bonfire then back at the general. His jaw was slack. He grabbed the general by the epaulets and shook.

"How could you? We're good as *dead*. The rebels could attack any second."

The blustering firebrand that had been General Wrathbone was gone, before the soldier stood a lame animal that knew its moments were numbered.

"All the gods on Olympus couldn't stop this."

He shrugged from the soldier's grip and began to walk back to his tent. Without turning, he called out;

"I suggest you take to your heels while you *still can*."

With that Declan was alone.

The chant had doubled in volume. He could hardly bring a thought together.

The night had turned cold and the intensity of the fire turned everything else into a black silhouette in his eyes. The shadows of the bewitched soldiers sawed back and forth at Declan's feet like jagged teeth. He shivered. The warmth promised by the fire seemed welcome now that he was on ground level.

The crowd didn't seem evil and mindless. He took a step closer and was half covered by the long shadows. He wouldn't be alone if he joined the circle, he wouldn't be afraid any more in the mass of men.

He could feel the power collecting, almost sizzling in the air.

It would be an easy thing to just give in and join in the horde. Even now he found himself humming along to the chant. He took another step closer. The shadows were up to his neck. What difference could one man alone make? How could he make it on his own if he deserted his comrades? It was so cold outside of the fire's burning red light.

There was a crack of a single gunshot. It tore through the night and made the soldier jump as though he himself had been shot. He quickly backed away from the circle and tripped over the discarded whiskey flask. The circle of men terrified him once more. He didn't want anything to do with this godless work. He drew a chain with a small silver crucifix from beneath his shirt and kissed it.

"Protect me, Jesus."

In a moment he was on his feet and running away from the fire. Up, over the ridge and past the dormant artillery.

He didn't look back when he reached the top.

# CHAPTER 12

*My sweet Rose,*

*I don't know if my last letter made it to you. I don't know if this one will. I'm going to write to you anyways. I miss you and it hurts. I didn't think it would. I been stabbed just last week and it didn't hurt like me missing you. I'm sorry that I don't have many words, but the ones I have I'm gonna send to you. If it wasn't for you, I'd have as many words as a mocking bird, and that ain't many...*

Samuel was used to dead folk, but not this many.

The letter he had written rolled through his head as he clambered over body after body, holding off the smell of new death and gunpowder with a camphor soaked bandanna. He had only seen two battlefields before this one, and he hoped to never see another that could match it. If it were not for the fact that he desperately feared for his life, he could not imagine pressing on past the first flesh wall of his fallen brothers.

He was nearly half way there. It would not be so bad once all the dead belonged to the enemy. Even now, a quarter mile out, he started to notice blue Union uniforms stick out of the sea of gray like sapphires in a blacksmith's dust heap.

He had thought that being a scout would be safe, easy work compared to infantry, but he had been wrong. Lord, had he been wrong.

Scouts were shot at, just the same as all the other soldiers. But when a soldier died in battle it was honorable. His family would get a letter from the commanding officer saying 'Corporal Suchinsuch, while protecting the freedom of these Confederated States, passed into glory...' and on and on. When a scout died folks would just spit and say good riddance. If he'd done his job well and good, he wouldn't be dead.

For scouts, it was like Moses crossing the Red Sea. Failure and death on three sides, all you could do was follow orders and keep on moving. He had been sure he was going to make it out alive before his first battle, when everything was drums and shining sabers, but he wasn't sure at all now.

It was night time and the field was black like the sky had come down and given it a kiss. To the north he could see a halo of light over a rise just after a creek. That was where he was headed, the Union camp. By the grace of God both sides had retreated to safety before there weren't enough men left alive to raise a barn. He had gotten used to stepping over the bodies now. He imagined they were big soft rocks, just moist with morning dew.

His mission was to get close to the Union camp and sniff out their reserves. Men. Guns. Powder. Shot. Neither side were firing their cannons now and the only thing he could hear were crickets and the whippoorwills soaking down in the creek. Samuel was unsettled by this, he should at least hear the dull roar that any large group of men make when clustered together. Something wasn't right. He hunkered down between a couple beat up hedges and took the field glass out of his satchel. It was cracked and wouldn't focus for anything, but it was better than nothing.

He couldn't spot a single man on the ridge standing guard. He swept the field with his glass but couldn't see anybody at all, at least not anybody alive. Some of the bodies seemed to shake and shudder, but he blamed it on a trick of the busted lens. The whole world danced when he looked through the thing.

The horizon looked like a black sidewinder in it. He had snatched it from a dead officer he'd climbed over earlier, hoping it would at least let him count how many working cannons they had when he got a little closer. He scanned back over the ridge and finally caught real movement. It was coming at him.

*Some nights when I'm lying in my tent and I can't sleep I think about the times we ran through your father's fields. I know he don't think much of me, but I don't hold it against him. I don't think much of me, either. Before I picked up this rifle and put on these grays I didn't amount to a hill of beans. I guess I'm worth two hills of beans now. My rifle is worth more than I am. That's what they keep telling me.*

A dark shape was briefly silhouetted at the top of the ridge, crouched down low and crawling like a raccoon. The figure tripped and rolled the rest of the way down the hill. It got up and splashed through the shallow creek and darted along the edge of the field, following the hedge apple row that the scout was hiding in. The scout collapsed the field glass and pushed himself up into a crouch. The figure was running at full steam, stumbling over corpses and rifles as it went. He wasn't on a mission; he was running like a hunted animal. The scout yanked his muddy bayonet out of its sheath and tensed his whole body. In his head he was whistling Dixie.

*It's like a coon's age passed since I signed up. I feel so old. Only two battles and I see Yankees like I see possum. Something to kill. I feel aged like old man McDermott. Beard a mile long. Nothing nice to say about nothing. I hope this war is over before there are too many more battles. I don't think I can live feeling much older than I do. It hurts.*

He sprung out just as the blue blur passed and hooked his free arm around the neck. The Union soldier choked and fell to his knees. The scout drew the knife back, preparing to stab the Yankee's stunned neck.

"Oh, I wish I was in the land of cotton-"

The man, with a power only one fighting for his life could muster, sprung up and smashed his head into the scout's chin. Samuel's head whipped back and the stars fell from the sky and danced before his eyes. He sat down hard and spat out the blood that was welling up in his mouth.

The Yankee twisted free and began to stumble away, coughing. Samuel's vision cleared and he spun on the ground, kicking up pebbles. He stabbed out at the retreating legs, but missed. The bayonet pierced through the Yankee's trouser leg and sank deep into the red clay, where it would not budge. The Yankee pitched forward with a yelp and slammed into the dirt, kicking his legs, trying to get free. In a moment the scout was up and on top of the man in blue who was croaking:

"Jesus, Mary, and Joseph! Don't kill me here!"

Samuel pinned the soldier down and barred his neck with a bony forearm. The Yankee had shaggy red hair and a sparse beard betraying his youth.

The scout hissed, "What are you runnin' from, you yellow sum-bitch."

The Yankee did not reply. He started to recite 'Hail Mary'. The scout grabbed his collar and bounced his head against the hard clay until he shut up. "Tell me why you was runnin' from yer own people, less I make yer shit-eatin' grin 'bout a mile wider."

The soft Irish brogue cracked as he replied. "They're doin' terrible things around the fire; things a man who wants to go to heaven shouldn't watch." The Yankee squirmed. "Please, let me go. I don't want anything to do with this war anymore if even the dead aren't safe."

The scout loosed his grip and spat some more blood into the hedges. He imagined Rose was watching over his every move.

"A-right, git." His words floated in steam in front of his face in the cool air.

"Thank you, Jesus." The Irishman started to stand up.

"That's not my name." said the scout. He yanked the bayonet from the ground.

"*Thank you.*" the Irishman whispered.

"Git!" the scout hissed.

The Irishman clutched his rifle in one hand and his pack in the other. He took two cautious steps backwards then turned tail and ran. The scout watched him fade from sight through the smoke of a smoldering crater.

He spat the last of the blood from his mouth and turned back to the enemy camp.

*I really hope the war hasn't hurt you none. You're back in Atlanta. You should be safe. I guess that is the only thing that makes me feel good about fighting. If I weren't keeping you safe I would have run to California by now. Don't tell nobody.*

As he drew closer to the ridge that hid the camp the glow grew brighter. The dead grimaces of the fallen soldiers glared up at him and cursed his path. The glow was an odd one, not of a hundred small fires, but of one great one. The eyes of all the dead picked up that glow and threw it back at the scout like it had rained silver dollars. He crawled low with his flank scraping the bramble bushes.

He was lucky that the scuffle, though quiet, had not drawn any attention earlier. A spotted scout was a dead scout. Once he reached the top of the ridge and saw what he needed, he could be back in his tent; he could finish the letter to Rose. She was the last thing he had that kept him human. Without her distant love flowing through him he would have gutted that Irishman like a pig, no matter what god he had prayed to.

He started to walk more carefully when he reached the creek. He hopped from stone to stone, crossing the water without a single splash, and started up the ridge. It was a steep hill. It was a wonder a single round from the artillery actually met its mark. The hillside was pocked with smoking craters from the day's earlier barrage. There was something special in the smell of the smoke, there was nothing else like it. It was the smell of crater smoke. Gunpowder and grass and dirt and meat all fuming together. The scout thought that this was surely what hell smelled like.

*I've felt a terrible burning since I left you. Not just the body burning like on a lonely night. But this new kind of burning. I don't know. I don't have a lot of words to use. What I have can't tell you how I feel. It's just a burning like I've never felt before. It's probably I miss you is all.*

He came to the pinnacle of the ridge and was dazzled by the bonfire that erupted from the middle of the camp. Who knows how many trees fell to fuel those flames, but it must have been many. The flames reached up and licked the sky with a light so bright it would make the moon jealous.

It hit the men circled around it and stretched their shadows out long and thin like railroad tracks all around the burn site. It looked like every Yankee in the county stood around that bonfire, and they were all holding hands and witnessing like a Sunday revival.

In the empty dirt between the fire and the circle of blue where three things. The first was a black man with no shirt. He had a shining blade in one hand and hair in the other. The second thing was a Confederate soldier, sitting quiet and still, but awake. The shirtless Negro held his hair tight and high. The third thing was lying on the ground at their feet.

It was a dead Union boy, half of him bloody, the other half burnt. There wouldn't be much to send home. The scout heard mumbo jumbo coming thick and oily out of the black man's mouth. He yanked up on the hair and brought the blade down to the neck of the Confederate and let out one last blast of gibberish so strong that the conflagration behind him leapt up and licked at the sky. He jammed the knife into the boy's neck with a scream. The black man yanked the knife back and held it high over his head, shining bloody and red. Blood spurted from the hole it left like whiskey from a shot gunned barrel. The Confederate slumped down onto his side, flopping like a landed catfish.

*I just want to tell you, I'm scared. But thinking of your face makes me strong. Don't tell nobody.*

The circle of blue boys was dead quiet now, holding hands and breath. The scout couldn't see any other soldiers. He crouched and scampered to an empty guard tower which he climbed up to get a better view.

Somehow in the scuffle his field glass had corrected itself. He was able to see clearly through half of the cracked lens. The black man was talking in his tongues again, slashing the knife at the burned Union corpse and spraying it with blood. He stuck the blade into the ground and lifted the dying Confederate soldier up like he was a sack of oats and threw him into the fire.

The flames picked up and took on a color of red that the scout had never seen before. The black man started chanting and the circle started to chant along with him, faster and faster until it sounded like a hurricane was flying over the camp. The scout started to shake, like the strange words were hitting him. The shaking made it hard to see what was happening down below, it turned the scene into a red and blue smudge. He twisted the glass and steadied himself until the scene came back into focus.

The scout started and almost dropped the glass over the edge of the rail. The burnt corpse was standing, crooked and twitching, and it was looking right at him. So was the black man, he was pointing and yelling. The scout snapped the glass shut and hurried down the ladder.

His boots hit the ground running and he didn't look back until he reached the top of the ridge. Nobody had fired a single shot and all he could hear were the huge logs cracking. The circle had opened up at one end and all was still but the one shambling figure working its way through the gap. The scout turned on his heels and flew down the ridge like a bat out of hell.

His foot sank deep into a divot in the hill and his boot twisted in a way it never should. He flipped over and rolled down the ridge, silencing his scream with tongue and teeth.

He landed face down in the creek and let its waters hold his pain. His rifle slid down the frosty, slick grass and butted into the side of his head, waking him up before he drowned. He grabbed the gun and scrambled across the water.

He twisted his head around and saw that he was only being chased by one figure. It was just a black silhouette with the glow of the flames. The scout knew it was the charred walking corpse.

It stumbled down the ridge in his direction, slow but steady. Samuel pushed to his feet and made his way across the battle field.

*Rose. I remember when we first met. You was singing a hymn and I was pretending to. But I didn't know the words and you caught me and smiled. Whenever I feel cold or alone I just think of that. I just think this war is a song I don't know the words to and I'm just playing along. As long as I know you know what's gonna happen I don't feel so bad.*

The scout was able to outpace the dead man, even with his fiery twisted ankle, but as he got closer to the center of the battlefield, the detritus of fallen soldiers and orphaned weaponry caused him to stumble and fall nearly every other step. Soon, his leg was so inflamed he could not bear to put any pressure on it at all. He was forced to crawl over corpse and crater.

He was panicked now, panting and praying as he scurried on. It seemed like the sea of bodies would never end, and he feared he would wear out before he crossed it. He looked back and saw a terrible sight that made him sit stock still. The charred corpse had one ruined arm held high, and it bellowed out a sound a healthy throat could never mimic. Smoke rose from the ground at the thing's feet. The scout was paralyzed. He looked closer. It wasn't smoke, it was steam. Sickly pink steam.

The steam didn't rise from the ground, but from the lungs of the dead that littered the battlefield. The steam started around the charred man's feet, but just as those bodies started to shake and shiver, the mist continued to jet from the reborn screams, radiating out toward the scout.

He forced himself up and ran through the burning pain in his leg, not daring to look behind himself again. He didn't want to be around when his boys started waking up.

*You remember that night we never went to sleep? I think that was my happiest night. Not when we were doing that thing, but after. When we just laid in the hay loft. Talking till the sun came up. That one always makes me warm. Like you was next to me.*

He was about a hundred yards away from his own camp now. He could see the Confederate fires lighting up the crest of the hill like a rising southern sun. He dropped his rifle and sped up for one last push. He hadn't gone three strides before something grabbed his bad ankle. He pitched forward and his face slammed into the cold clay. He kicked as hard as he could, but it wouldn't let go. The grip tightened and he could feel the shattered bones in his ankle grinding against each other. He twisted around best he could to see what was holding him back.

"Brother, brother, you came back." What clung to his leg was a pile of Confederate, like something you would find at the back of a butcher shop. It was a wonder he was still alive, there wasn't much left.

"It's been so cold waiting for you, brother." He spat more than spoke. The steam hadn't reached him yet, but he was already a monster.

"Just... help me back to the medic." He coughed and dark red blood shot from his mouth. Even if the scout weren't crippled, it would be impossible to get the heap back to the medic. He didn't have anything like a bucket.

The scout winced and twisted further around, until he could reach his sheath. The steam was so close he thought he could smell it. The howls of the dead flew past him on the midnight air and echoed off the rise, riding round to smack him in the back of the head. He wrenched the bayonet loose and brought it to the side of the soldier's head.

"I'm terrible sorry."

"Terrible-" said the mess of man, but he couldn't finish. The rest of his words gushed out of the gash the scout drew from ear to ear. With each crimson pulse the grip grew weaker until the scout was free.

But it was too late.

They were waking up all around him, and he was painfully slow. He crawled toward the light over the hill, but the hands of the dead started to reach out and snag on his clothes like the twisted branches of a winter hawthorn.

He was very close, he could make out the confused shadows of southern boys dashing up and down the fire line, calling out orders that made as much sense as the painful wails of the army of the dead that was rising.

Soupy red clouds had covered the sky and blocked out the moon. Everything had turned to shadows, even the scout's sharp eyes couldn't pick out anything more than movements and reflections. The shine of a dark eye, the flash of copper buttons, the glow of yellow-white ivory teeth.

The teeth were in his face, he could smell their rotten breath beat on him from all sides. The teeth were at his legs, his arms. He still had the bayonet out. He started by stabbing but that didn't do much good, so he began using the heavy brass butt of the thing to brain the shuddering abominations. As he fought, he saw the quick flash of firelight on ten oiled barrels. His boys were pushing the Gatling gun they had captured to the fire line. The scout could fight his crippled way from a cluster of biting corpses, but he stood no chance against the fury of the Gatling gun. That thing was pure hell fire.

He dredged up what little strength still hid within him and tore from the groping hands, smashing skulls left and right with the butt of the bayonet. He pushed to his feet one last time and strode and leaped like a jackrabbit over the shaking bodies and sharp, biting teeth. His legs pumped mindlessly, on fire and glass and blood and bone. He screamed like a madman as he charged up the hill. He heard the clink of bullets being dumped into the hopper of the Gatling. He saw the thin silhouette of the artillerymen crouched around the alien machine. *Click-click-click*, the bullets dropped into their chambers. He was halfway there.

Click. Click. Click. That was six barrels loaded, any second the spinning barrel would start filling the air with lead. Boys were rushing to the line now, taking a knee and taking aim.

"Don't shoot! Don't shoot! Don't shoot!"

The scout shouted with the last bit of wind left in his lungs. He was just a floating head now. He finally came to the crest of the hill and stumbled over his own boot.

He rolled, over and over, down into his safe camp, but he did not feel safe at all. The gunnies hadn't started firing yet and the riflemen stood their ground. The scout rolled to face their questioning gazes. The men at the Gatling gun stood in awe at the sea shambling toward them. All the scout could hear them say was;

"It's a miracle!"

"Is that Willy out there?"

"…they're all *back!*"

The scout screwed his eyes shut, the pain all over him was sinking into his bones like he was being lowered into a boiling pot.

"This ain't a miracle! It's the goddamn rapture!" The scout was breathing fire, it felt.

They stared at him still. He couldn't bear to keep his eyes open anymore, the light hurt.

"Shoot! Shoot! Shoot!"

The scout buried his face in the ground, and let the war of sound wash over him like a Mississippi flood.

*Pam! Pam! Pam!* Went the great Gatling, its forty five shot tearing all in its path like sheets hanging out to dry. He remembered Rose, how beautiful just hanging out the washing could be, when she was the one doing it. *Crack! Crack!* From the Parker and Richmond rifles. He heard the squeal of artillery wheels begging for grease. Then the *Pom!* of the cannons firing grapeshot. The boys were giving it all they had, but the scout didn't feel like it would be enough. He rolled onto his back, still blind with pain, ready to stab at anything that threatened him and his people. He screamed and writhed so that the heavens could hear his pain. It was all he could do. He was just a scout.

*I know your daddy doesn't think much of me, especially since I'm only a scout, but I do my best. You can tell him I'm the eyes of the company. I'm the hound that scares up game.*

He opened his eyes and the whole line was floating in a haze. The gun smoke clouded everything past five yards. The Gatling gun was nothing but a firecracker shooting at a thunderstorm. He was pained on his left side, and rolled over, hoping the cold dirt would slow the throb a bit.

Then, through the haze and the pain came the crisp crunch of squared heels. A clean, un-scuffed pair of boots walked to the scout.

*Tell you the truth. The only reason I signed up was to show your daddy that I was man enough to take your hand.*

"Git 'em up!" hollered a voice the scout knew too well. Unforgiving hands grabbed under his armpits and yanked him painfully up, his lame legs dangling. He squinted his eyes open and immediately dropped them to the dirt. It was General McMurtrey.

"Jus' what in the blazes did you see out there, scout?" His face was fire red from whiskey and duress.

The scout couldn't raise his head to talk, he was too tired. "The dead walkin', sir. The dead walkin'."

The General spat. "Fine! That's jus' fine!" He shook his fist at the air. "Gimme all you got you son of a bitch!"

The scout slumped heavy in his own world of pain. "The head's what stops 'em…"

The scout was swimming now, so he couldn't see the General screw up his face.

"Throw this yellow dog to the medic, an' git all our boys to the front. I'll be damned if some crippled conscripts git the best of old McMurtrey!"

The shining boots dwindled off and one of the arms started dragging the scout toward the inside of the camp.

The last thing he remembered hearing was- *Hup! Hup! Hup! Eastside! Fire at will! Hup! Hup! Hup! Westside!* The click of an empty Gatling gun, and shouts of, 'Ammo! Ammo! Ammo!" The last thing he thought, before he blacked out, was that it was funny how war made people say things three times.

*There's one thing I want to ask you. I need to ask you. I have to ask you. But I won't. I'm gonna ask you that question when I get back, whether the war is over or not. I'm going to ask you that question and I hope the answer is yes. It would be yellow to ask it in a letter, especially since I don't know if I'm gonna make it or not. Blazes, it doesn't matter. Even if I get torn to a million pieces tonight, I'm going to ask you, one way or another. Mark my words.*

He came to on a red dirt floor, floating down at the feet of a soiled medic who was cursing and thumping the chest of a man on a table. The white tent, it had been white, was filthy, and it seemed blood had found its way into every fold and crevice. The medic thumped one more time, cursed and spat. He rolled the body off the table, to join the other corpses on the floor. The freshly dead man was another medic, a minnie ball through the chest.

It was funny, how a lump of lead the size of a marble could make a hole the size of a mason jar. There were a lot things that were funny about war, but not the kind of funny you laugh at.

"Oh Jesus," Said the medic. "It was hard enough when I had help! What am I gonna do without you, Jeb?" He braced himself against the table and lowered his head in a swoon or a sob.

The scout couldn't make much sense of anything anymore; it was like the devil was playing fiddle in his head. The screams of the living and the howls of the dead encircled the tent, rifles popped off like forgotten fireworks. The big guns were silent now.

It wouldn't be long.

A bullet whizzed through the flimsy tent and one of the hurricane lamps exploded, sending oil and glass every which way. The medic snapped out of his funk and stomped out the wick before it could ignite the stinking slick. His face was puffy and pink, like he was fresh from a shave. He couldn't have been more than 18. He looked down at the scout with his drooping hound dog eyes and said;

"At least I can fix you, friend."

The medic scooped up Samuel and hauled him up to the table. The scout started to scream as he was dragged out of the calm stupor he had drifted into, back into the flames of reality. The medic looked at the boot angled astray, flopping with convulsions, and pinned the scout down with arms and elbows. Samuel couldn't sit still; he was swimming again, this time in a sea of agony.

With some effort the medic was able to strap his legs down to the soggy table with the stiff belt that was bolted to its side. He disappeared below the table as the scout writhed and came up from the corpse pile with a filthy rag, which he jammed into the scout's mouth.

"Just you wait a second," He grabbed a jar from a dented foot locker at the base of the bed. "I'm gonna help you with that pain."

He snatched a stained handkerchief from his pocket and tilted a bit of the clear liquid onto it. He moved to the scout with it, but at the last moment, held it up to his own face first. He inhaled deeply and reeled, catching himself from falling with an awkward hand on the table. He giggled like a half-wit.

"This isn't so bad at all!" the medic slurred. He tilted forward and pressed the powerful smelling rag over the scout's face. His shocked body took in the fumes in quick, shallow breaths. His pain started to numb, so did his mind. His whole body started to float away, piece by piece, until he was just a floating head on the table, staring up at the medic.

The medic stumbled and drunkenly yanked the boot off of the scout's twisted foot. They both heard the sick pop of bone and gristle, but neither seemed to pay it mind. The war of noise outside seemed to float underwater. There were groans outside the tent flap; twisted figures were painted in black on the spotty canvas, wandering aimlessly. Rifles still cracked, but they seemed far off, like hunters in the wood around the cabin the scout was raised in. He remembered the days he had spent with Rose, and the nights.

He was settled with dying, but he wanted her to know what happened to him. He wanted her to know that he wasn't just a scout, he was a man.

The medic rifled through the tray under the table and brought out a dark leather belt, which he tightened around the scout's afflicted leg. He disappeared from view again and came back up with a squared off saw, covered in dirt and gore. The medic spoke haltingly as he wiped the thing clean on his sleeve like he would an apple.

"Don't you fret 'bout the foot, brother." His big pink face wobbled close to the scout's. "They got some fake feet now that a lady wouldn't tell from real."

He laughed hysterically, his breath reeking of the stuff from the jar. The scout saw the walls of the tent shaking now, twisted fingers of shadows pulling at the tie-downs and the flaps. He saw a three-fingered hand push through. It sounded like they were laughing too. There are a lot of things that are funny about war.

The scout didn't hear the gun shot, neither did the medic, it just busted through one side of the tent, through the medic's head, and out the other. The medic stood for a moment with a dumb smile on his face as a little fountain of blood flowed out his ear. The medic dropped to the ground without a sound as the walls started bowing in. It must have been close to sunup, because the whole tent was glowing pink and red. Someone, a preacher maybe, had told the scout when he was a boy that these were the colors of life. The scout thought that it was funny that he only really started seeing these colors when he was about to die.

A gleam came to the scout's eye and he said, "One last thing." He said it to himself and he said it again and the tears started to rip through the canvas and the red light shined in and the crabbed up hands started to pull the whole thing apart. His own hands, dumb like a baby's, were busy in his pockets and at his neck.

He found the pot metal chain with one hand and the letter with the other and ripped them both loose in a spasm as the pain started throb back. He bit down on the rag and dropped a thin gold ring, chain and all, into the envelope. He folded it up with shaking fingers and checked one last time that he had spelled the address right. He had always been terrible with spelling.

One of the dead was in there with him now, now two. He held the letter up to his lips as they closed in and imagined that he was kissing her paper white neck. He stuffed it under the lumpy cushion of the table. Face to charred up face he stared at the dead man before him and he said, "One last thing…"

And he remembered the last few lines he wrote in that letter, as the claws and the teeth and the blood became all he knew. He thought of the letter, and he thought of his Rose.


*Just remember that I will always love you. No matter what. I don't think this war could stop us. I don't think the devil could stop us. Even if I have to wait a hundred years in heaven or hell for you. I will. I love you Rose.*
*Samuel*

*Dearest Samuel,*
*I received your last letter, the one you wrote just after your second outing. I am very proud of your penmanship, and you shouldn't slight yourself about spelling, you will learn in time. You may think yourself dumb, but just because you are awkward with your letters does not mean you are not a bright boy. You are my bright boy, no matter what father says. I hope you are safe, I know you are. I just received word that your regiment had terrible losses to some new Yankee gun or such, but I just know you are alright. I know that the second things turned sour, you were running. There's nothing to be ashamed of, this war isn't civil at all. I can see you now, running with those powerful legs of yours. I can see you running over hills of grass, under sun and moon, until you are back in my arms…*

# CHAPTER 13

Declan had been almost relieved when he was captured by the rebels. Now that he was locked in the cage at the brig tent he felt safer than he had running over the horrible battlefield, glancing back to see the terrible fog lift from the ground. Feeling his stomach sink as the earth seemed to shiver. He was glad to be away from that, even if it meant being in the hands of the enemy.

When he came upon the enemy camp he tried to circle it, protected by the dark of night, and for a short time it had seemed he succeeded. He made it past the camp and into the safety of the woods. He would have been free if he hadn't stumbled into an inky hollow where two soldiers were committing a sin that he tried not to think about. He had been so shocked that he was unable to pull his rifle on them; he could only stand slack-jawed. The dry dead autumn leaves rustled and scraped at their knees with the back and forth. The one on the bottom let out a strangely pained little mewl as their unloosed belt buckles clinked in rhythm.

In his youth, Declan had the horrors of the sin drilled into him by a clammy priest whose eyes would linger uncomfortably long on the boys of the parish. It still gave him nightmares.

The soldier on top spotted Declan, despite his carnal ecstasy. He pulled a pistol and quickly stood, tugging up his trousers.

"Don't you move a goddamn muscle." He hissed, then he changed his mind. "*Turn around.*"

Declan held up his hands and turned his back to them. He heard the other man talk.

"What're we gonna do, he saw-"

"He didn't see a cotton pickin' thing. Ain't gonna say anythin' either."

Declan heard the pistol cock. He bolted.

"Hey!" The man shouted behind him as Declan zigzagged through the trees. The pistol barked, the flash casting his silhouette on the foliage. He could see the trees break ahead of him, the relative lightness of the open field. He didn't see the party of soldiers until he burst from the woods.

In an instant a half dozen rifles were pointed at his chest. He was on his knees, hands above his head by the time his pursuers blundered out of the forest. The man who seemed to be in charge berated them.

"Eustace! Thorpe! What in the blazes where you doing away from your post?"

"Huntin' down this here spy, sir. Found him snoopin' around in the woods." The soldier panted.

"Why were you in the woods?" The captain's scowl couldn't decide between Declan and Eustace.

"Heard somethin' queer." Eustace looked at the ground and scuffed his boot in the dirt.

The captain squinted at Eustace. "Alright-" He spat. "We'll take the prisoner. If I find out you two have left your post again you're going into the brig along with the Yankee."

"You should probably just shoot him, sir. Save you some trouble."

"Are you telling me what to do?" The captain took two swift steps forwards until he stood nose to nose with Eustace.

"No sir." His voice shook.

"Then keep your damn fool ideas to yourself and guard this flank. Spies are more useful to us alive than dead," He squinted at Declan, "For a time."

Declan was stripped of his pack and rifle. A bayonet at his back guided him toward the light of the Confederate camp. His lips moved and he hoped the lord could hear him praying.

The cell was roughly twelve by eight. Declan reckoned that six stout men could lift and tip it over, but his only companion in the cell was a blind drunk captain that would grow blusterous if Declan disturbed him on his pile of straw in the corner. The brig tent wasn't much larger than the cage, housing nothing but a stinking bucket just outside the cell and stool upon which the jailer sat nodding. Declan had been stripped of his belongings, they lay in a heap in a far corner. He couldn't keep from pacing, though he hadn't been locked up for long. The confinement stretching the minutes into hours strung tight in his mind like mandolin strings. They thought he was a spy, and Declan didn't tell them differently. It seemed like the lie would extend his life. He never thought he would long for the ghetto of Chicago where his mother had shriveled and died, but war did strange things to a man.

The brig tent was at the far end of camp, away from the firing line and the rows of big guns. It had been quiet when he had been jabbed into the cell, but now in the distance he heard the traveling roar that was a messenger all too often of many men in a panic.

Declan felt his false sense of security melt away as his hackles rose. He began to pace furiously. He nervously rubbed at the bruises on his neck from where he had been clotheslined earlier. He was thinking of the Negro in the circle.

The Fire. The Fog.

He remembered, before the orchard had failed, when he was in the country, his father had allowed him to keep a rabbit as a pet.

The critter had wandered into the barn and cornered itself, vibrating with fear like only a prey animal can drum up. Declan had put it in a wire chicken cage and fed it well and petted it, taking care of it until it finally trusted human touch. He named it Finny.

Declan remembered a week after the apple harvest failed that terrible year. The cage being empty one morning. The strange shriek from the yard, heard but not seen. The gamey meat for dinner. The forlorn but somehow jovially sinister grin on his father's leathery face as they chewed on the sinewy stuff.

"Sure, Decky, but it's a shame your little pussy ran away. Probably hopped off to someplace where there's actually some damned food!" He laughed in that horrible way that punched Declan in the chest. Declan gave his share of the meat to his brothers and just ate taters. He tried not to eat any meat ever since.

Declan shook the bars of the cage, but they wouldn't even reward him with a sound. They just were.

The tent flap was thrown aside. Eustace's head jutted in, looked back and forth, his body followed. The jailer snorted and stood at the disturbance.

"Everything is tight as a barrel here, what can I do for you?" He rubbed the sleep from his eyes.

"I'm, ah, I'm supposed to relieve you. They need men at the front." said Eustace. He hardly took his eyes off of Declan.

"Why me and not you? This's been my duty for a week."

"Legs crippled, fell under a wagon last month. They don't want me fightin' and we're short on men." He gestured at his leg which was twisted, pigeon toed out and bent. "You'd better get moving or there'll be hell to pay."

Somewhere at the front the cannons began to roar.

"Fine, fine. Here's the keys. If'n I find out your chiseling me I'll make you regret it. Never thought I'd see the front again."

"Just ask Captain Giraudoux if you don't believe me."

The jailer swung his rifle over his shoulder and stormed out. Eustace tied the tent flap after him and turned to the cage. He began to twirl the keyring on his index finger.

"What's your name, pervert?" His eyes were tight with hate.

"Pervert? I saw you earlier-"

"You ain't seen shit." Eustace's face was so tense it added twenty years. A pistol appeared in his hand at his hip. He started circling the cage.

The drunk was snoring. It didn't cover the swelling waves of panic that washed over the tent from the firing line. The cannons sounded like fireworks. The tent stank of the bucket.

"That how you have your fun? Peekin' in on people's private business?" He picked up the bucket.

Declan knew he couldn't say anything to remedy the situation. He could see the madness in the other man's eyes.

"Filthy little rat!" Eustace tipped the bucket and splashed it into the cage. Declan narrowly dodged being soaked by the putrid stuff.

"Think you're so much better than me." Eustace kept circling slowly, his eyes never leaving Declan. "You can't make me feel bad. Nobody can. Not you, not my daddy, not, not... *him*." His eyes squeezed shut, trying to dam the tears that turned his face red.

The gunfire was whizzing past the tent, the hollering of soldiers swirled close. The cannons had ceased. Eustace didn't seem to notice.

"Listen- I don't think you're-" Declan started, stepping over the drunk to the far side of the cage. The gun was wavering in Eustace's hand. Tears were streaming down his face. He snuffed back his running nose.

"You can't think anythin'! Goddamn-priest-fucking-Irish-pervert, who're you?" The words came out in gasps as he tried to stop sobbing. He snapped the hammer back.

"*Who're you?*" Eustace bellowed.

Declan dove to the floor just as the pistol cracked.

He landed with his nose an inch from the sickening puddle and pushed himself back up, hunched low and ready to skitter and dodge the next shot. Eustace was grunting through gritted teeth, but not making any sense. The shot woke the sleeping man, who stood slowly and belched. He held his sea green head.

"Eu... Eustace? What're you doin?" He stepped closer, noticed the gun. "What the hell is that?"

He followed the barrel to Declan. "Who... Hell, I don't care. Put that damn gun away right now, private! I won't have you shootin' an unarmed man in a god-damned cage."

A bullet buzzed through the tent causing all three of them to duck.

"I don't have to listen to you." The tears had stopped, replaced with a bitter resolve.

Someone ran by outside screaming, *To arms! To arms!*

Eustace's face was plastered with a terrifying smile that bore only the worst auspices of humanity. He stepped close to the cage, his arm jutting between the bars.

"I don't have to listen to anyone anymore."

"This is your last warning-" Screamed the captain, but he couldn't finish. The pistol bucked and all was silent but the high pitched whine in Declan's ears. The captain fell back, blood gushing from his neck in sick gurgles.

Declan saw his chance and he took it. The killer's arm poked through the bars and into the cage. He dashed for Eustace's outstretched arm and it felt like he was moving in a dream, pushing so hard with each step, floating airborne for hours it felt between strides, the pistol slowly, so terribly slowly, pivoting toward Declan.

He could see that the thumbnail that was pulling the hammer back was chipped badly, and every cuticle on the hand was torn and ragged. There was nothing left in Eustace's eyes but the horrible yellowed whites. Declan reached out for the arm, stumbled forward, all his weight pushing it in the wrong direction, twisting it back against the bar of the cage farther than it should go.

His ears were still stuffed with cotton, but he felt every snap and pop in the man's bones. The pistol dropped inside the cell.

Eustace fell back silently screaming with hard breaths, landing on his ass and kicking at the dirt with his heels. His ruined arm flapped at his side. Declan snatched up the pistol and pointed it at the screaming man.

"I'll kill yah! God! *I'll kill yah!*" Eustace pushed himself up. He reached over his shoulder and struggled to swing his rifle to front. It kept catching on his broken arm making him cry out.

"By god! Huh! By god, I'll kill yah!"

"Don't do that- *don't do that!*" Declan had the pistol trained on the man's head. Eustace had the rifle to front and was trying to work it one handed.

Something began thrashing at the tied off tent flap. Eustace turned just as it tore through to the inside.

"Thorpe? Aw, god, Thorpe, what did they do to you?"

The other man Declan had seen in the hollow stumbled in. He had been shot at least four times, one of the bullets tearing his side mercilessly, leaving nameless organs on display. He walked as a life-sized marionette would. His once toothsome face was locked in a grimace. With the wounds he had sustained there was no way he should be up and walking.

Thorpe limped toward Eustace, arms out seemingly for balance. Eustace backed away shaking his head.

"What's *wrong* with you? Answer me..."

He tripped over the bucket and tried to catch himself with his bad arm. He landed, howling. Declan pointed the pistol at the two of them, transfixed. He felt like he should shout something but knew it wouldn't do any good. Thorpe groaned and fell to his knees next to Eustace. He started tearing at the soldier's uniform.

"Thorpe! Not after... We were... God! Help!" Eustace thrashed at the grisly man ineffectually. His uniform was ripped open and within moments it seemed his flesh was coming off just as easily under those strange puppet nails.

"Mercy!"

Declan couldn't stand to hear it any longer. He shot Thorpe once in the back, but still the carnage continued. Declan was shaking terribly, making his next shot miss. There was so much red between the two men it was difficult to tell where one ended and the other began. It sounded like hell within the tent and it sounded like Armageddon without. He exhaled and fired the last round.

The emptiness that filled the air afterward sounded like white light.

The bullet struck Thorpe in the head and cast brain matter against the canvas of the tent. He slumped to his side twitching, and then was still.

Declan dropped the pistol and held his head, feeling as though it too might explode, trying to understand what had just happened in the last five minutes. He shared the tent with three dead men now, and from the sounds outside he knew more would await him.

But Eustace wasn't dead. He spoke, voice high and breathy like a man exulted by opium.

"I just wanted…" His throat was torn. He coughed and spat blood. "I'm not a bad person."

Declan got down to the edge of the cage. "Give me the keys. I'll pray for you. Just give me those keys." He reached out through the bars but couldn't quite touch Eustace.

The dying man reached into his pocket sluggishly, his face was blank, eyes wide as was his mouth, like he was beholding something far greater than himself.

"Lord, don't judge this boy harshly." He had a finger hooked through the key ring and withdrew it from his pocket, then was still.

"Wake up! Wake up, man!" Declan shouted as he stretched far as he could, his fingers scrabbling in the dirt.

Eustace was no longer with him. The keys were only a foot away from Declan's straining fingers. There were fires burning outside the tent. He could smell the smoke, even indoors. It wasn't the smell of a cooking fire or of lanterns, but the burning cotton and sundries and blazing tents. He looked around the brig, nothing was on fire, but the flickering light from outside cast shadows on the tent walls of people running or staggering by.

The gunfire was heavy. He stayed close to the ground and no longer jumped when bullets screamed by overhead. He picked up the pistol once more and grabbed it by its hot barrel.

Trying to remain calm, he reached out with the hooked handle and began raking at Eustace's dead hand. With each stroke he could see the keys pull free a fraction of an inch. Overextending his arm to reach so far barely gave him enough leverage to exert any pressure.

He gathered all of his will and slammed down on the hand.

He groaned. The finger had let go of the key ring, which still glinted halfway out of the pocket. He threw the pistol in exasperation and felt about himself for anything that would help. They had stripped him of everything but his clothes, all pockets bare; they had even taken the little cross from around his neck. The canvas of the tent was being scratched from outside, and the dozen bullet holes in it burned like limelights. He was sure he hadn't much time left.

"Holy Mary, mother of God-"

The belt was still about his waist. In a moment he had it off and was casting with the heavy buckle at the gleaming ring of keys. The buckle's hook was small but found purchase on the dead man's hands more often than not. His panic rose with the war that was running past the tent, and so did his inaccuracy. He had never been any good at fishing.

Again and again he tossed the buckle, pulling slowly on the belt, hoping to catch the key ring with the tiny brass hook. There were lines in the dirt between him and the corpse that resembled a dense musical staff.

He forced himself to slow down, even as he shuddered and heard a man screaming bloody murder outside. He acted like he had a rifle to his shoulder, breathed deep, exhaled, and released. Finally, the buckle caught the keys and he gingerly tugged them from the pocket. With one more yank the keys jangled within reach. He grabbed them and hastily slid his belt back into place.

But he was surrounded now. The tent shook. The lantern swung back and forth from all of the flesh pressing on the dingy canvas that made up the walls. Here and there butterflies of blood bloomed across the coarse material. He heard them screaming now that his focus was broken. He dropped the keys twice trying to unlock the cell as twisted arms began to reach through the gaps in the tent. He could hear the poles creaking under the stress.

He turned the key the wrong way on the first try. He cursed as the tent heaved around him like a gasping lung. Finally the lock snapped open, but the door would not budge. Tears of rage burned Declan's eyes as he gritted his teeth and put his shoulder to the door.

There was someone tearing at the flap to the tent. Hand, arms, all crimson, reached in. He pressed as hard as he could but he didn't have it in him to budge it. He backed up and jumped into it, achieving only a wicked bruise and a flat, resonant gong from the bars.

Screaming, he ran to the far side of the cell. When he turned for one final charge he saw there was one of the mad men in the tent. The man was screaming, too. Declan didn't stop to think, that part of his mind had hidden from the madness, he ran and took flight in a bum-rush that slammed him into the door. It sounded like an oversized tuning fork when he hit. He rolled over his shoulder and landed on his back, boot-heels kicking into the dirt just inches from where his pack and rifle lay.

The horrible looking man didn't seem to notice. He only turned slowly and began walking toward Declan. There was something wrong with his foot and it popped sickeningly when he put weight on it. It sounded like someone grinding hard corn. The man was still screaming, it looked like he was scared by something on the ceiling.

"The light! The light!"

Declan scrambled to his rifle. It was still loaded. He aimed at the man.

"I don't wanna shoot a sick man!"

"White light!" There was a pain in the man's voice Declan hoped he would never understand. He continued to shamble toward Declan.

Declan shot him in the face. The man fell backwards, limbs still twitching and reaching.

"Holy Mary, Mother of God-" Declan tried to recite the prayer as he shouldered his pack and snapped the bayonet onto the rifle. He couldn't get past the first bit because he got too choked up. His eyes stung salty. He just kept saying that fragment. It hurt him to say it because it felt like lying.

He ran out of the tent and into hell.

The camp was aflame, everything lit up like the moon was sick and burning itself out.

Not one thing stood still in the close, choking smoke.

Men ran in and out of the clouds, shooting, chasing, screaming, all of them made monsters by their wounds and terrified faces. The sulphurous gun-smoke burned his nose. He charged into the madness, the gleaming tip of his bayonet his compass point.

The blade found a target before Declan knew there was one. In the first opaque cloud he ran into a woman, a beautiful negress. Her apron was filthy with blood, one strap ripped at her shoulder, exposing a heaving breast. She had run herself through on the bayonet.

"Daddy!" The woman gurgled through the blood that welled up from within. Her face was pretty and terrifying all at once.. She shuddered and charged down the blade. Declan's mind reeled at all as all of his sensibilities were assaulted. He swore and kicked her back before she got within reach. One of the woman's arms reached out with grasping fingers as the other hand tugged at her wild hair as though she were trying to rip her own head off.

"Back, woman!" Shouted Declan. He thrust out with the rifle to ward the her off, but was pushed from behind. The blade slid into the woman's throat like a finger poking into a pie. She fell, her mouth opening and closing stupidly. Declan thought of the pumping lips of a landed bass.

Unseen hands grabbed him about the neck and squeezed. Declan couldn't breathe. The drowning fish was still front and center in his mind. The madmen had similar eyes to the fish, he realized. Eyes that moved, but did not live.

Every bit of his body pulled for air. He brought the rifle up and slammed the hickory stock into the side of his attacker. Each strike did nothing to loosen the grip. The fire in Declan's eyes was growing dim.

*New Moon.* He thought absently, looking at the swirling sky. The pink mist had arrived.

He felt down the barrel of the rifle and snapped the bayonet free. The jerking of his choking body fed into his arm as he stabbed behind his head. The sound of the mayhem around him swelled into one large murmur in his ears. He could tell the blade was scoring, but it was glancing off of something hard.

Just before the red curtains came down and completely obliterated his vision, the blade struck a soft spot and sunk in, stuck in place like he had jammed it into a patch of mud.

The hands released his neck, but grabbed his shoulders, pulling him down with it as it sank.

Declan didn't know how long he lay on the ground, sucking air hungrily. It could have been a minute, or it could have been a year. It was like the time his brothers had lifted a jar of ether from the apothecary and they had taken turns sniffing the evil liquid from a red bandanna until they were sweating the stuff. That night had been one long laugh. This night was the opposite. His brain felt larger than his skull. He spun drunkenly to his feet. His legs still didn't feel like they were his own. Below him he saw the man who had choked him. The face was ruined, caved in on one side, the bayonet stuck ferrule deep in the temple. His back was arched, mouth open, the tongue stretched out like he was trying to taste the dirty pink sky.

Declan felt something leave him as he placed the heel of his boot on the man's jaw and wrenched the bayonet free. He couldn't take a full breath no matter how hard he tried, and the air he got was smoky and sour. He saw the knife clutched in his hand, the rifle grasped in the other like a club.

He didn't have it in him to clash with any more of these things. Even though they were wild and inhuman, it still felt like murder when he killed them. How many were there? Was he the last sane man? Was he even sane? Why would a loving god allow this happen?

Declan knew he was sane, because he was running from the maelstrom like a spooked rabbit.

# CHAPTER 14

Declan nearly tumbled out of the tree when he awoke. He had dozed off plenty of times amidst the boughs of the apple trees back in his family's orchard, but in the months since he had enlisted, his body had lost the knack of balancing in the branches and grown accustomed to his cold, lumpy bed-roll.

His bed was miles behind him, he recalled. His legs were sore and knotted from his panicked flight away from the unholy conflagration back at the Union camp and the escape from the Confederate cell. He breathed deep and gripped the tree to steady himself. He was woozy as the waves of memories washed over him from the night before, like that terrible fog.

The foliage was thick and he couldn't see through the tight blanket of leaves in any direction but down. From the glance he allowed himself it looked like the fog hadn't followed him into the woods the night before. He felt safer up in the trees, always had. His father couldn't climb a tree when he was drunk.

It worried him that the forest was silent. He cupped his palms around his mouth and let out a bird call, as he had often done as a child. The only reply was a '*Weet! Weet! Weet!*' Off in the distance, receding. It sounded like more of a warning then a happy response.

The tree he was in was tall, taller than the surrounding ones. He decided to climb higher; partially because he wanted to see what was going on, mostly because he felt safer the higher he got.

He climbed up and around the difficult trunk. It was nothing like the apple trees of the family orchard, it was much more of a challenge, there were almost unreachable gaps between branches and fewer places to stop and rest. He reached as high as he could without hugging it and shimmying up the old trunk like a lumberjack.

He shielded his eyes against the rising sun and nearly dropped off. The whole time he had been climbing he should have been running. Above the canopy he could hear the distant pops of the rifles, he could feel the screams. He could see it.

The damned fog.

Before him, miles off past the tree-line, was a field he barely remembered running through. It had been slick and dark in the chasm before the sun bloomed, and it had been quiet. He had thought he was safe, and he had been for his tiny collection of winks up in the tree, but the fog had caught up with him and brought the hellfire of war with it.

Rolling slow over the green pasture, the fog was a light pink. Like the mist that leaps from a man's chest when a bullet runs him through. The image was cut into the theater of his mind and as he clambered down the damnably high tree, the few moments played over and over.

"Oh, love. Oh, love." He gasped the whole way down- his mind unable to call up any suitable prayer. He had seen men running from the mist, some plunging from it amid the muzzle flashes that lit it up like lightning.

Like all ponderous things, the mist seemed to move at a crawl from afar, yet it kept close at the heels of the soldiers. Seeing that huge thing stretch across the horizon filled him with a feeling he had only had once, back in the orchard when he was small.

His brothers were cutting down a sickly old tree and a rotten bit of trunk had crumbled unexpectedly. The tree began to topple in the wrong direction. It was everything little Decky could see. It felt like he was falling up, slowly. Had his father not yanked him out of the way by his coveralls it would have been the end of him.

That tree seemed like a small thing now, even the war did, compared to the mist.

He reached the lowest bough and was faced with fifteen feet of bare trunk. He didn't remember how he had climbed it in the first place. Getting down on his knees, he hugged the bough, looking close for and knots he could have used as handholds.

It would have been impossible to have climbed up with his nails alone. It was too far to jump.

There was a noise off in the bushes. Declan froze and peeked over the branch in the direction of the commotion. A man came stumbling through the undergrowth. He clutched his shoulder, and his head was down like he wanted to ram whatever got in his way. His bad leg left a line behind him in the dead leaves. When he came to the tree Declan was perched in, he hit it full force and was knocked onto his back with a scream that was more a gasp.

The man lay there breathing hard. Declan could see that he was badly wounded and his leg was turned at an unnatural angle. His service pistol was clenched in the hand that was pressing down on the oozing wound. His gasps seemed to be made of words, only making sense to the man himself, and maybe to his creator.

Declan was about to call to him, but before he could there was more rustling and another figure emerged into the hollow. He looked like he shouldn't be standing, let alone striding as he was. He was Union by what was left of his Uniform. It looked like he had been standing next to a powder keg when it had been lit off. Declan fancied he could smell the charred flesh even from his height. The man's arm dangled at his side as though it was forgotten, and his nose was missing altogether. He looked to be a senior officer by his neatly trimmed salt and pepper beard. His spectacles had been broken and it was plain to see the the glass had burst his eyes. A hideous, sightless, terror. Declan hugged the tree like it was his mother.

The crippled man on the ground saw the bloody mess coming for him and screamed. He aimed and fired the pistol twice into the Union man's chest, but it didn't slow him down. The shots made holes, it looked like, but they did not bleed as they should. Without word or sound, the hideous man in blue bent over and started tearing at the cripple with tooth and nail. He had the feral movements of an animal. The trees did little to mute the horrific screams of the man as he was ripped asunder.

Declan pulled the bayonet from its sheath and flexed it in his hand. His heart was pounding in his head. He knew how he was going to get out of the tree.

He didn't let himself think twice about it. He slid around the branch and hung for a moment by one arm, said a two word prayer, and dropped off.

He landed boots down on the burnt man and his bayonet whistled after. In one movement he plunged the blade guard deep into his back before the force of the impact sent Declan tumbling off in the leaves.

Landing on the man had softened the blow, but the wind had been knocked out of him when he landed. For a moment all he could see was the sunlight breaking through the leaves of the trees, and the way each little spot of light seemed to flit and swirl like silver fish darting to the surface of a murky pond. He gulped for air but his chest refused to open up.

The Confederate still lay on the ground not far away, sputtering and kicking up loam with his boot-heels. Declan was able to roll himself over and take little sips of air to chase away the darkness that had crept into his vision. He started to crawl to the man, who he saw was in the worst of shape.

The burnt up man had torn the gray uniform to shreds and a fresh gash had been opened on the soldier's neck. By the time Declan got to him the kicking had slowed and stopped. The man's body relaxed and his eyes calmly gazed at the roof of the forest, probably catching sight of those fish.

Declan closed the man's eyes when he stopped breathing. He began a halting Lord's Prayer, finally able to take a whole breath.

The ordeal left him numb and his dry tongue tried its best to stick to the roof of his mouth. He felt the urge to cry, but he had gotten that under control after he saw his first battlefield. The prayer made him feel better. It reminded him of a time when the world made sense, when he thought he understood himself. He reached for the silver cross that had hung from his neck, but remembered it had been taken from him when he was captured.

Before he could say amen, he was grabbed by sharp fingers on his shoulder. He felt the cold wet scrape of a beard on the back of his neck. He yelped and sprang forwards over the corpse with all of his nervous energy and was free. He spun and pushed himself into a tightly wound squat.

The burnt man was lying on his belly where Declan had just prayed, blood drooling from his mouth in gouts that made his beard glisten.

The bayonet was still stuck in his back. Declan felt bile rush up and burn his throat. He reached behind his back and tried to bring the rifle off his shoulder, but the strap was caught on his canteen, which rung hollowly with each attempt.

The burnt man gurgled and pulled himself over the dead soldier. It looked like his legs weren't working anymore. He crawled toward Declan with shocking speed, his jerking movements and the cold emptiness in his bloody eyes brought down a loathing on Declan the likes of which he had never felt. In two blinks it would be on him, tearing him to bits like it had the cripple.

The rifle would not budge.

Declan sprang to his feet and backed away, still wrestling with the rifle. As he yanked at it he heard something tear and it was finally free. He leveled it down, cocked the hammer and pulled the trigger. The Spencer cracked and the crawling man was still, eyes wide and white, just five feet from Declan.

The man smelled like he hadn't just passed, but had been dead for some time. He cautiously stepped closer, cranked the lever of the rifle to chamber a new round. The blood of the man wasn't flowing; it was thick and dark like strawberry jam. This man had been dead on his feet. Even then, as Declan drew close, its jaw flexed open and closed, ready to bite him if he drew too near. This was no longer a man.

Declan had no trouble firing directly into its skull. He got dizzy when he wrenched his bayonet from the thing's spine. Through the trees he could hear distant pops and screams. He would once again have to run. He searched the dead soldier, stripping him of the navy revolver and a pouch with all the works for it.

He made the sign of the cross over the body.

"Lord, pray tell, what have you done?"

He left the hollow at a short lived run, which faded to a winded jog that not even the devil at his heels could have sped up.

He was exhausted, body and soul. He hadn't eaten anything but the hardtack and stew that had been served for lunch the previous day. All of the strangeness and panic had driven the hunger from him. Even as he jogged through the woods, the void in his stomach was dull and easily ignorable throb, but it was getting harder to put one foot in front of the other. If he turned his head too quickly a wave of giddiness would crawl over him.

By the time he penetrated the other side of the forest, the shrouded sun above pointed to noon and all he could muster was a plodding trudge. He was glad to be out in the open so he could see if he was being chased, but on the other hand the war-torn fields were a shooting gallery and he was an easy target to any man that happened to be hiding in the rubble. He stayed low and slunk through the fearful field like a raccoon.

He passed a ruined wagon and panicked, diving beneath it and breathing hard until he reassured himself that he hadn't gotten turned around and wandered right back onto the field he had run from. A similar fear took him after he dusted himself off and continued. He came across a corpse in a crater and fired twice into it without stopping to think, the lever loading and hammer cocking in one smooth gesture, lubricated with fear.

The corpse hadn't moved, nor did it now. It was acting as a corpse should, as did the rest of the bodies Declan saw as he clambered across the ruined landscape. Acres turned to miles.

The sun was setting, letting him know that he was traveling roughly north, though he still had little idea where he actually was. His mind wandered. He thought of the madness he had seen in the last forty eight hours.

He thought of the Negro that had taken over the Union camp, and he wondered why he himself hadn't been controlled in the same way as the other soldiers. He wondered if it was because of his religion, or the cross he had worn, or if it was because he had been on the edge of the camp up in the tower when the dart ritual had taken place. He wondered if the fog was going to continue to spread, if the dead would continue to walk, and if he would ever be able to stop running.

Was it was the rapture? From the looks of the charred prairie he walked through, the world had already ended. He passed burnt out farm houses surrounded by blasted fields and tried not to think about what happened to the families that had lived in them.

The sun was halfway set when he finally came across land that wasn't torn and scorched. He picked his way through the overgrown crops that soon blocked his vision. The corn had never been harvested and had burst with silk that did its best to pull at his clothes and blind him.

He pulled off an ear with the hopes of having a bit to eat, but as he shucked it he saw it was thick with white mold. He tried a few more ears as he walked and they were all glued with the stuff.

The corn was confining, higher than his head and planted close. He began to panic as the sky grew dark, with no way to know if he was almost out or walking in circles. The smell of the rot was everywhere; it was beginning to turn his stomach.

Red winged blackbirds flitted from hidden hollows to peek at him, shout *conk-ra-lee* and fly off as he approached. Declan wished he could just for a moment fly up over the corn like them and get his bearings.

He had noticed that many problems in life don't seem so bad when you can see them from above. He yearned for the forest, or at least for some trees.

It was dark with only a wash of orange sunset above his head when the corn finally gave up. He wasn't expecting it, blundering out onto flat dirt and glimpsing a house.

He jumped back into the corn and crouched, taking in the civilization before walking into it again. The area was so cuspy, the owners of the house could make him dinner or make him dead, depending on which side of the war they supported. He wished he wasn't wearing a uniform.

He sat watching until the stars came out. It looked like the house was abandoned. There wasn't any smoke in the chimney, no lamps had been lit, a clothesline was bare and dangling. There was a fresh grave just before him, where the corn broke.

Its only marker was a tarnished copper vase half buried in the mound, filled with wild flowers and a well-loved rag doll. Maybe the family had fled when fighting drew closer, or they had left for greener pastures when that white rot took the corn. Declan crept from the field staying low, just to be sure.

"…pardon me for the evil I have done on this day, and if I have done any good, deign except it, watch over me…" He prayed below his lips, just in his throat. He looked up to the stars for solace but he saw more black emptiness than light. A shiny blackness like a dead man's eyes.

He slowly climbed the stairs to the porch, failing to keep it from creaking and popping, each noise making his heart race. It excited him just as it had when he would sneak out of the house at night as a child, expecting the noise to wake his father and unleash the hell of penance that would follow.

As he reached the door no lights glowed in the panes and no feet paced the floor. He couldn't hear anything but the dying breeze in the corn leaves and the whine of an unseen weather-vane that couldn't make up its mind.

The mat was askew. The door was not locked or bolted and opened without a sound. It was totally dark inside, but it smelled human, like someone still lived there. Something was wrong. Before he could back out, there was a hard pressure at the back of his head and he heard the hammer of a gun cock.

"Take off your hat when you're indoors." said a flat, female voice.

He was frozen, face slack and dull.

He still couldn't see anything. The hard cold thing pressed the back of his neck harder.

"Go on, what did your momma teach you?"

He slowly reached up and removed his hat, holding it in front of him like he was at church.

"You plan on using that rifle?"

"No… no, ma'am. I just wanted a place to sleep."

"Deserter?"

"No, ma'am! I'm still in service to the Union, but my company went mad-"

"Shush. *You* went mad when you signed up. Here, take two steps and turn 'round. Need to see what kind of coward you are."

He did so and turned. She stepped forwards into the faint light that drizzled through the doorway. Her spectacles caught the light, wisps of unrestrained hair just turning grey making a halo about her face. Just below were framed the gleaming tunnels of the scatter-gun's barrels. He twisted his cap between fretting knuckles.

"You can't even be twenty. How old are you?"

"Eighteen and a half, ma'am."

"Do you love your mother?"

"I did, ma'am, like breathin'."

"Shush. That's enough." She lowered the shotgun a bit and looked at him over her spectacles, eye to eye. "Can I trust you and that nasty rifle in my house?"

"Aye! I'll even unload her, God's my witness."

She lowered the shotgun and uncocked the hammer.

"I don't mind the rifle, but you can leave God outside."

He didn't know quite how to answer that, so he just said, "Thank you, ma'am."

"Come in the kitchen, can't spare the last bit of coffee on you, but I have chicory."

His eyes had adjusted to the murk and he saw the rest of her. All in black, her hair down around her shoulders. Her lined face. She must have been in her forties. She smiled at him, but it was still mostly a frown. Her eyes looked like they weighed as much as cannonballs.

"Thank you, grandmother."

"I *ain't* anyone's grandmother."

\* \* \*

The kettle crackled on the stove and he sat where he was told. The kitchen could have been any color. It was impossible to tell with the windows covered and the lamp turned down so low it might as well have been off, making only orange flickers in the few things in the room that still shined. The spoon on the table. The door knob to the back porch. Her spectacles, tilted down at the flame.

"Haven't had any visitors since your brothers came 'round the beginning of the month." Her long fingernail tapped the glass of the hurricane lamp.

"I'm sorry, ma'am?"

"The soldiers. They came through on their way to kill some people, I'm guessing." She stopped tapping. "They took my horse to pull one of their wagons and left me with a sick mare that died the next day."

"I'm sorry, ma'am." Declan was filled with some strange urge to rip his cap to shreds.

"You apologize one more time and I'll turn you out."

He nearly apologized again, but caught himself.

"Yes, ma'am." He could tell by how excited the kettle sounded that it was about to whistle.

"So where are you headed? Where do deserters run to, pray tell?"

"I don't rightly know. I'm not sure where I am. Are we closer to Springfield or Louisville?"

"As the crow flies, Louisville. Though, you'd have one hell of a trip on foot."

"I'd walk here to hades if I knew the war couldn't follow me."

The last bit was drowned out by the cry of the kettle. She lifted it off the stove and let the water drizzle into the coffee pot.

"What's your name?" She said, without turning.

"Declan Moirey. Private first class." He parroted this as he had often before. The army had re-taught him his name.

"And yourself?"

She put the pot down on a pad of woven corn leaves between them on the table.

"Catherine. Cornbread?" She produced a well wrapped parcel from a cupboard.

"Thank you, ma'am."

The bread was dry and tooth-chipping like the hardtack they were fed at camp. He softened it in his chicory and ate sloppy bites of it. His hunger made it taste amazing. As they sat in silence he resisted the urge to ask for another piece since she hadn't offered. Off somewhere in the house a clock chimed off ten hours.

"So, you live out here alone?"

"Didn't use to. Had a family."

"Where are they?"

Her glasses glinted then shifted down. She hid her mouth behind her mug.

"No longer with us."

It made him want to cry or pray for her, he wanted to do something, but had no idea what.

He thought of his mother being all alone in her final days, husband dead, one son at war, the other two prodigal and useless, nobody to take care of her when that damned cough started bringing up blood. He felt like he had to apologize to Catherine for something, for everything. No amount of prayer before bed made him feel any better about this. Even his most sincere prayers rang hollow with each repetition.

He didn't want to see this happen again. He didn't want any mother anywhere to ever be alone again.

"You shouldn't stay here. The war's gettin' close, ma'am." A shiny beetle was crawling across the ceiling above them; Declan followed it with his eyes. "I could help you to the next town. You can come back when the war's over."

"You think the war will end?"

"Of course, ma'am. All wars end."

"They don't end. The men that run them just change the name."

"Not sure if I follow."

"Wouldn't expect you to."

There was more silence. Her chicory was nearly finished. He saw her efficiently remove a small vial from somewhere below the table and silently count out a dozen drops into her cup. Laudanum. He couldn't see the beetle. He was afraid it was above him, ready to drop into his cup.

"You must really love this place."

"Nope. There's nothing left to love about it. I just don't care to leave. Could burn to the ground tomorrow and I wouldn't care."

"Sounds like the last years have been hard..."

He trailed off, remembering the looming mist that lay somewhere past the field and forest, possibly within it by now. He knew it was getting closer. The fog was the kind of thing that always did the opposite of what you wanted it to do, like a house-cat or a delicate plant. He was so weary his bones felt hollow, but the fear of the fog had propped his eyelids up with bloodshot veins. She didn't answer him; she tossed back the last of her chicory. His tongue moistened thinking of the tart little drops of oblivion.

"So, you have some laudanum, there?" He cocked his head at the cup.

She stood and brought their cups to the sink.

"Yes, I have."

She picked up the lamp and walked to the door.

"I'm going to sleep and so should you. You can bunk on the rug in the living room. There's nothing left of value, so I don't expect you'll steal anything." She walked out the door and left him in darkness with the sound of her skirts swishing off. He heard her talk under her breath, her voice choking toward the end.

"There's *nothing* left."

He made his way slowly to the rug and stretched out on it. The windows were covered, and he was thankful, otherwise he wouldn't have been able to resist staring out of them. He set his pistol at his head, rifle at his side, pack at his feet. Laying down felt grand, as reclining can do after a long day of hard work; but he couldn't keep his eyes closed.

He felt that every second he rested, the fog spread closer and he knew his rifle wasn't fully loaded.

When the clock struck one he sprang up and pulled the curtains aside. All was quiet and dark, the moon casting only a rarefied gauze over the yard and the grave and the rotting, moldy corn. Even this reassuring glimpse didn't settle his spirits. He sat back down on the rug and began cleaning his rifle, action by action; loading up seven rounds in the stock. He tried to sleep again, but awoke with the twin chime of the two o'clock hour. Another peek through the window may as well have been a painting of what he had seen last. The wind was so still that even living things looked dead. He paced to the ticking of the unseen clock, learning to avoid the creaky boards in the old floor. He could feel the warps through his worn-thin soles. He took up the revolver and felt the works, loading from the little pouch of powder and shot, twisting-clicking-snapping every bit that would yield beneath his fingers.

He tried to sleep, but awoke with each chime of the clock.

He lost track of the hours, spending the rest of his night sharpening the bayonet, keeping pace with the ticking clock. He eventually and truly fell asleep, but it didn't feel like it. He dreamed he was lying on his back, staring at the ceiling, waiting for something terrible to happen.

He awoke to a jingling in the front yard the next morning. Catherine was busy in the kitchen, so he took it upon himself to investigate. With pistol drawn, he slowly opened the door and peeked out.

A huge shape snorted wetly in his face, making him jump back.

There was a horse on the porch.

*  *  *

The horse was in sad shape. Its flanks were scratched raw. The bridle was twisted like it had been tangled in something.

The saddle was crusted with dried blood. Its black hair was dusty and matted. There was an infinite sadness in its dark eyes.

"Look at you, then." Declan held out a hand and the horse tentatively snuffed it. It grunted and lowered its head, presenting the dirty white strip that ran from muzzle to mane. He stroked it gingerly and the horse pressed into his hand.

"That's a lad, there now. Where's your owner?"

Declan stepped out onto the porch and began preening the dirt and burrs from the animal's coat. One of the saddlebags was torn and empty, but the other was intact, holding some ammunition and a bundle with pemmican and hard tack. Declan pulled a twig from its mane and it whinnied, hooves clumping on the boards of the hollow porch. Catherine appeared from within the house.

"No horses on the porch." she said.

The horse grunted.

* * *

Declan fed and watered the horse in the barn. He began calling it Ulysses as he cleaned the last of the dust from its coat. He thought it was a fit name for a traveling companion, and its face somewhat resembled that of the general which bore the same name. Asides from farming equipment and tools, there was also a beaten, but serviceable, wagon in the barn. The faint odor of rotting meat permeated the place, and after searching for the source, he found it outside.

There was a dead horse, torn to bits here and there by scavengers. It was halfheartedly covered with dirt; the shovel lay in the tall grass a few yards away as if thrown. He crossed the lawn to pick it up, but stopped when he reached it. He could see out over the cornfield all the way to the forest in the crisp morning air.

The sky above the trees was thick and rosy pink. He picked up the shovel and stood, using it to hold himself up. He frowned at the sunrise for a time, then crossed himself and went back into the house.

She had cooked up a pone of corn and it sat between them with a pot of chicory. The windows were covered, but the sheets she had nailed up were translucent enough that Declan could see the dull surfaces of the kitchen. It was clean; at least where she seemed to cook regularly, the rest had a young haze of dust. Above the door leading to the back yard was a nail surrounded by the faint outline of the cross.

"Thank you kindly for the hospitality, ma'am. I owe you sun and stars." He eyed the pone in the black iron skillet.

"You're welcome." Her face was still stone, her eyes were down and stayed there. She poured the chicory into crockery cups. He was glad she didn't make eye contact; it almost hurt when she did.

"When are you moving on? I can't spare much more charity."

"Hopin' to get out soon, but..." He wanted to tell her about the mist but wasn't sure how to.

"Spit it out."

"I saw your cart was still in good shape." He wanted to tear into the pone with his bare hands, but he waited to be served.

"You can take it if you want. I've no use for it." She took up a jagged bread knife, its handle was burned like it'd been left on the stove.

"No, no! That wasn't my meanin' a'tall."

"Then what was your meaning?" She cut into the pone, dull tip of the knife tapping the skillet bottom as it walked through the cake.

"I was thinkin' we could load a few of your things into the cart and take you into town." He paused, not knowing how to describe the menace that crawled just over the horizon. "There's something terrible coming this way."

She lifted a chunk of pone and dropped it, steaming, onto his plate.

"Dandy. Can I take my daughter with me?"

"Ma'am?"

"If I'm just goin' to lift up move out, I should take my beloved with me, shouldn't I?"

"Didn't know you had a daughter, ma'am."

"Sure I did, had a grandson for five minutes, too."

Declan looked her square in the nose for he couldn't bear to look her in the eye. He nodded, knowing a sad story would follow. His stomach made him grab his chunk of pone and chew it as solemnly as he could.

"I've been alone, as a woman, for damn near five years. Had my daughter, a few hands to help on the farm, and my daughter's beau."

"Umm?" A fine snow of corn atomized from his mouth.

"Six months ago," She continued, "He ran off to war, hoped to send money back to us to help through this bad harvest. Few weeks later, Milly started to show. Money stopped coming in the post a month later, then the letter saying Joseph had perished at Antietam." She paused, her mouth a sour little slit. Out came the little vial again and she counted out ten drops into her chicory.

Declan's pone was gone; he pushed the crumbs together into a pile and pinched them up into his mouth with his fingers.

"Bless you, ma'am, but that's horrible."

She sipped her chicory and dabbed at her mouth with an ivory napkin.

"Mhm. It was. Milly was destroyed by the news. Wouldn't leave bed. Her stomach started troubling her and it took everything for me to get her to drink a glass of milk. I'd dismissed the hands when the rot spread through the field, so it was just us two out here. Doctor Thomas came around once or twice to look at her, said it was a toxemia she had. He said he was gonna come back with medicine, but he never did. The war got too close for him, I guess."

Her voice began to waver and he could see the red rings rise around her eyes.

"Then… *you people* took my one horse. Left me with a nag with hoof and mouth. You people…"

She stared trembling at him, took a long sip from her cup and cleared her throat.

"Without a horse, I couldn't take Milly to town when she took a turn for the worse. I did my best to take care of her, but I'm no nurse. One night the baby started comin'. By the time I had boiled the water she was gone, and the little one passed in my arms shortly after, he…"

She took off her spectacles, tears squeezed from between her tight eyelids.

"He was so beautiful. So... So... So..." She allowed herself to sob twice then sniffed and stood. She turned her back to him and walked to the window, wiping her eyes.

"I haven't anything left."

She hunched over the sink basin and sighed.

"Truth be told, if you'd come an hour later I wouldn't have been around to greet you."

Declan thought of the fresh grave in the yard and tried to imagine the slight woman digging it.

"I'm so sorry. That should never happen to anybody." With her back turned he reached out and grabbed another hunk of the pone.

"I'm glad I came when I did, the lord is merciless to suicides. It's a sin-"

She spun and shouted. "Don't you tell me what's a sin! You're a goddamn murderer for *hire*!"

She put a hand across her mouth and turned back to the window. She sighed.

"I'm sorry. You didn't kill Joseph. You didn't steal the horse. You didn't..." She put her spectacles back on and wiped a swath of dust from the window.

"Somebody's comin' through the corn."

# CHAPTER 15

Declan had been rapt by her outburst, and now that it was broken, he looked down to see that the pone had crumbled in his reflex-tight fist. The chair skidded over the floor behind him as he stood up and dashed to the window. The corn was shaking in straight line and parting like water around a fish.

"Mother Catherine, you should get in the cellar. You got a cellar, right?"

"I ain't hidin' from some desertin' soldier like you. You can both go on your way for all I care."

"Not sure if that's a soldier, ma'am. Let me, eh, let me talk to him." Declan's boots pounded the floor, on into the front room to retrieve his rifle. He heard her speak from the kitchen.

"Tain't a chance in Hades he's settin' one filthy foot in this... oh, he's wounded!"

Declan was jogging back.

*"Don't let 'im in..."*

A window crashed and the widow screamed. Time seemed to slow down once he heard the window shatter. It was nearly as though the shards of glass hung in the air, slowly spinning jagged fairies. She was frozen, hands up covering her face in shock. A gnarled hand reached through the broken window.

The glass cut as it passed, small but bitter gashes. Then Catherine was grasping her wrist, and the bloody hand through the window grabbed it as well. She was pulled over the sink, her knees catching the edge of the basin, keeping her from being pulled any further.

Declan had the rifle up, cocked and aimed, but there was no way he could take a shot without hitting the woman.

Time oscillated, speeding for an instant with the kettle drum thrum of his heart beating in his temples. Glass still spinning. He couldn't seem to turn the rifle around fast enough, then snap! He had it in both hands above his head, ready to bring the stock down on the dead man's head. Then it whipped through the air, whistling the same pitch as the woman's infinite scream. He hadn't choked up on the barrel enough, the butt whacked off of the window frame above and the vibration shocked his hands.

Slowly he saw the rifle fall as his hands burned and popped. A flash of steel caught his eye as time jumped forward. The cocked rifle struck the floor and discharged, he only heard the first fraction of the pop, then the cicada whine screeched in his ears and drowned everything under muddy water.

A moment of silence.

A series of daguerreotypes.

Catherine's eyes, wide and wild, inches away from the bared teeth of the bloody man.

Steel. The bread knife still in her hand.

A silver blur at the thing's wrist as she saws.

The hand, retreating, limp, ropes of meat catching on the jags of glass.

Sound began to return to the kitchen.

"-out! Son-of-a-bitch! Filthy, filthy thing!" Catherine was trembling with rage.

Declan grabbed the rifle and levered another cartridge.

"Are yah hurt?"

She didn't answer, just kept swinging the knife at the window and hollering. He grabbed her around the waist and pulled her back to the far side of the kitchen.

"Stay back, stay back, now." He kept the rifle on the empty window. All was quiet but for Catherine's breathing and the tapping of a ladle swinging on its hook. He moved slowly around the table, glass crunching under foot. There wasn't any sign of the thing.

"Do yah have a cellar?"

"You can only get in it from outside." Her voice shook.

"Go somewhere safe, then."

He heard her skirt swish as she left, the thock of her thick heels going up the stairs. He got as close to the window as he dared, but there was no sign of the thing. He lifted the sash of the back door slowly and saw only the yard through its window. Backing into the living room, he retrieved the revolver and bayonet, which he locked into place on the muzzle of the rifle. He could hear Catherine walking about upstairs, doors opening and closing.

Glancing out the windows showed nothing. He passed through the kitchen and out into the yard.

Outside there was a bit of blood by the window but no other trace. The smell of the dead man was still on the air, mingling with the rotten corn on the slow breeze. His chest was tight and every zephyr that cut a path in the corn made him jump. Maybe the terrible smell wasn't from the one walking corpse, but from thousands, waiting just out of sight in the corn, waiting for the one moment he turned his back.

It was impossible for him to face the corn at all times, as he was surrounded by it. He hated corn fields. This sort of thing wouldn't happen in an orchard. Anything can hide in corn.

He made a full circuit of the house, finding nothing. He was about to go back inside when he heard something from the direction of the barn.

Ulysses was whinnying.

He ran.

The sun had risen above the trees behind the mist, bathing everything in unnatural pink. Declan's cap blew off and he made no effort to retrieve it.

The first thing he saw as his eyes adjusted to the dim barn where the twin white orbs of the horse's eyes, rolled up to the rafters. Ulysses was spinning in place, head twisting around, legs bucking.

The dead man had halfway mounted him, a leg and an arm over. It was growling like its voice came straight from gurgles of its stomach. It was tearing at the horse's mane, its mouth biting at the neck.

Declan saw that there was no chance of a shot and dropped the rifle. The shovel was leaning against the door where he had left it earlier. He snatched it and made sure to choke up.

"Oh, love. Oh, love..." he panted as he walked to the fray.

He raised the spade like a scythe and shouted at the thing, to no effect. He prepared to swing once, twice, stopping just short each time because the horse's terrified head would swing directly in the way.

Declan screamed as though it were he that was being devoured. His feet shuffled one way and the other, not knowing what to do.

In another moment, an idea burned into him. He jammed the handle of the shovel in the path of the horse's approaching leg and gripped it, bracing himself.

The handle snapped before the horse's shin, but it was enough to throw it off balance. Ulysses toppled over and crushed the dead man beneath its bulk. The thing snarled and clawed at the horse, only it's head and a hand free. Ulysses was struggling to get up, making Declan work quickly.

The snapped handle of the shovel left it as long as a town-ball bat. Striking it smartly with the broadside did little but disfigure the screaming face, but three solid whacks to the throat with the edge finally silenced it.

Ulysses was up and clambering to the far corner of the barn. Declan was relieved to see it looked like the horse was unharmed asides from the bites and scratches. He looked down at the dead pile at his feet and knew he couldn't leave it with the horse. It would be cruel. He dropped the shovel and grabbed the fallen by its muddy boots.

It was slow going; the creature had been a big man, nearly twice the size of the Irishman. The thing's neck yawned and flopped from side to side, bumping off humps in the dirt. At first Declan tried to look away from it, until he realized it didn't bother him. The war had changed him from the farm boy he had once been, but the last few days had twisted him immensely further. Shooting at real men, looking back, seemed more natural and innocent than hacking an abomination to pieces. That thought made him confused. He didn't know how he should feel. The corpse seemed to shrug in response as he dragged it.

He rounded the corner of the barn and stopped. He slowly let the dead one's boots down and took the revolver from his waistband. The dirt pile had been thrown aside. A dead one was hunched over the rotting corpse of the horse, devouring it.

It was fresher looking than the others Declan had seen. The only clue that it was one of them, aside from its current meal, was a large dry blood stain on its back, surrounding a gunshot wound. It had been a young rebel soldier, a bit shorter than the Irishman, but athletically built. It hadn't noticed him, too busy feasting on the gore. Declan raised the revolver and took aim.

All was still. The corn ceased rustling. The click snap as he pulled back the firing hammer was far too loud.

The dead one heard it and jumped up, gore flinging from its stained mouth. Its icy blue eyes burned with a horrible intensity. It screeched and charged Declan just as he pulled the trigger. The bullet slammed into its shoulder, throwing it off balance, but in a blink it was barreling toward him like a cannon ball. Declan skipped backwards, fired, scored a blow to its gut near where it had caught the first mortal wound.

Still it charged on, fingers clawing the air between them. Declan pulled the hammer back for another shot, but something jammed in the works. He swore, turned, and ran. It was just a few yards behind him now, running with the terrifying speed of a man possessed.

Declan ran around the corner of the barn, towards the door. His bayonet and rifle both lay in the dirt inside.

Sharp fingers grabbed him from behind before he could enter.

He was thrown to the ground. The dead one jumped on him and slashed at his face, its eyes rolled back and mouth gaping in an oily scream. Declan threw his arms up and was able to deflect the blows, but he knew he couldn't keep it up for long. The thing had a knee on his chest and it was getting hard to breathe.

He tried pushing it off, but couldn't get enough leverage. The pistol was still in his hand, his finger pulling at the jammed trigger automatically. When he caught an opening in the flurry he jabbed the gun into the thing's unprotected belly, the barrel sliding into one of its wounds.

The dead one shook and coughed up an unbearably foul smelling ichor, which hit Declan's chest with a nauseous splat. The combination of the smell and the lack of air sent his head reeling. His vision began to blur as more blows landed. His cheek opened up, he felt, and his nose, but the pain was pulling back. He almost felt like he was stepping out of his body and watching the action from above.

The horrible thing on his chest, staring at the sky and howling like it was necessary to live. Its arms just blurry arcs of Confederate gray crowned in crimson. The autumn sky fell, turning to speckles of blood that dyed the dirt around him. Everything came into a surreal focus. Declan felt he could count every brown hair on the thing's head.

He knew it was still screaming, but the world had taken on a muffled cotton mute. It was all going slowly. Everything was so light. Head. Heart. Hands.

Its eyes were white. Its teeth were red.

The sky. The sky. *The sky.*

The eyes disappeared just before he let himself slip into the warm light. The weight was off his chest. It felt nice to not feel.

* * *

He had silk thin slivers of a dream where he was being shouted at by a rotting rabbit carcass when he woke up. He was wet and cold, spluttering on his side. He saw the bucket that had no doubt splashed him. The time before his sleep came back to him and he screamed, rolled over and kicked out his legs into the dirt, his heels scooting him backwards.

"Stop it this second!" a voice scolded, "You're alive. You look awful, but you're alive."

At hearing a proper human voice, Declan stopped thrashing and looked around. It was Catherine.

"Moon and stars, but you stink! I have half a mind to fill that bucket up with lye and douse you again." She kneeled down, knees popping like a thawing pond. She picked up her shotgun from where it laid.

"What's the matter with those men?"

Declan had trouble answering, his heart was racing from waking back into the nightmare. He couldn't breathe and talk at the same time.

"They're not... men. They're... monsters."

The dead one lay on its back a few feet away, the top of its head blown clear off. Declan pushed himself up and started probing at his face.

"Now you owe me for your life, as well as room and board."

"Thank you ma'am. I'm sorry you had to see that."

She didn't reply, just walked back to the house.

\* \* \*

The shadows of morning had retreated into their sources, maintaining the slight slant of the mid-day autumnal sun. Declan had been pacing the kitchen for half an hour, telling his story to Catherine. His cap rested on the muzzle of his rifle, which leaned against the wall next to a broom. The slugs and powder from the revolver sat scattered on the table, the revolver clicked and snapped in his nervous fingers. He couldn't find what had caused it to jam. Catherine stood at the sink, gazing through the broken window.

"I'll say I wouldn't have believed you if you'd told me last night, but I guess I don't have a choice now."

"Will you come with me, then? We haven't a chance in hell if we stay here much longer."

"I told you already, I'm not leaving. Here is a good enough place to die as any." She twisted a dish rag in her hands, "Nothing to live for."

"O, if yer so ready to die, why'd you fight back earlier?" The bread knife she had used was still sitting in the sink.

She was silent for a time; she dropped the rag into the sink and sat down at the table.

"It was just reflexes, I suppose."

"*Bollocks!*" He stopped and composed himself, apologizing with his eyes. He continued more quietly.

"I know you don't actually want to die, and if I hear you go on about it again I *will* leave you here so those devils can take you, like it or not."

"My family is dead! I have nothing but this house and forty acres of smutty corn-"

"I've seen dozens of men die in the last few months, stepped over the bodies of a hundred men I've called brother."

He reached into his pocket and took out the letter. He shook it and slapped it down on the table. "My mother is *dead*. I just found out before all this." His voice was quivering with a kind of sad rage.

"Do you know what I have waiting for me if this war ever ends? A grove of dead apple trees and a couple no good brothers too deep in the drink to take care of their sick mother."

He took a breath and his eyes went wide for a moment. He crossed himself and murmured. He looked to the window then back at her.

"I'm not going anywhere without you, Catherine. You've got some living left to do. Both of us do."

"I'm not leaving my daughter, you can shoot me first." She was looking at her hands, folded and trembling on the table.

"You're some grand ass, you know that?" Declan sighed.

"You're a boy with a gun."

The clock ticked. Declan snapped the revolver open and sat at the table. He began cleaning and reloading it.

"Could I have a bit more of that pone?"

"It's dry."

"That'll do."

She grabbed a plate that had been left on the table earlier, still crummy. The knife crunched into the thick crust of the pone.

"What was your daughter like?"

"Sweetest girl you ever met. Made the best apple pie. Don't know where she got it; I can't cook for two licks."

"O! Really, now? You must be mistaken, for my mother made the best apple pie."

The clock continued to tick, but they couldn't hear it because they were talking.

# CHAPTER 16

The only good thing about nightfall was that they could no longer see the advance of the fog over the cornfields. Declan had tried to divine its movements as he made his rounds of the property, wetting his finger with spittle and holding it aloft, hoping to catch which way the wind was blowing. The weathercock on the roof was silent and his moist finger refused to tell him a thing. The air was still all that afternoon, yet the fog continued to billow closer.

Ulysses had been unapproachable at first, shrinking to the farthest corner of the barn when Declan had first come to collect his dropped rifle, but after a dozen visits the fear seemed to leave the horse, and the offer of a mealy apple from the kitchen's cupboard seemed to erase the last few doubts Ulysses had about the Irishman.

The rounds were dull, but tense. Declan's mind imagined shambling horrors around every corner. He even fired wildly into the corn after he thought saw a stalk shake, scaring a blackbird so soundly that it left a white streak as it flew off.

Declan was glad that they seemed safe for the time being, but a part of him just wanted that stained and torn army to show up and get everything over with. He hated that part of his mind, but not as much as the wheedling little voice that told him he should jump on Ulysses and ride, hot as a fever, to any town that would take him.

As the sun sank and all grew dim Catherine hollered at him from the windows of the house until he resignedly went back inside. She said it was for his own safety, but he felt a small twinge in her voice that made him think otherwise.

The cupboard was open in the kitchen when he walked in. All that remained in it was a sack of corn meal and a half empty jar of what looked like bacon grease. She was beating some yellow glop in a chipped crockery bowl.

"O, no, ma'am. Don't cook up more pone on my account. I've got some pemmican I can eat on."

"Who said it was for you?" She began to guide the mush out of the bowl and into the skillet. The fat she had greased it with refused to mix and created a rainbow ring around the rim.

"Fair enough." He stood nervously for a moment and went into the living room. He gnawed on the pemmican as he peeked through the windows one by one. It was getting dark in the house again. He checked the lock on the front door then made for the stairs, but he stopped mid step, looked about himself, and found a chair of the right height. He wedged it up against the door handle before proceeding once again upstairs.

There were two rooms and only one looked lived in. Declan was thankful the other one was dark. The bed stripped of its linen and the dusty bassinette made him feel as sick as any scene from a battlefield. The smell in the room was altogether wrong. He left shortly after looking in. Ghosts followed him.

The other room was obviously Catherine's. It was spare, with a small wardrobe, a washbasin, and a wide bed that had visibly sunk on one side, as though there were an invisible weight upon it. The floors were thin and creaked.

He could hear Catherine slam the grate of the stove downstairs below his feet. He walked to the one window and pulled the curtains aside and tucked them so they would stay out of the way.

Through it he was able to see out east, over the fields, to the distant rim of the forest where the moon was just beginning to hit the fog and paint a pink halo on the very highest branches of the trees.

There was still no wind. Declan imagined what it would be like to be a sailor perched atop the crows-nest of a tall-ship beset by still seas. Feeling the madness that comes into a man's eyes when there is so much nothing to look at.

But, suddenly, there was.

Off in the distance, just where his vision lost focus, there was a wavering smudge in the green of the field. As it drew closer, Declan could see more clearly. He could see the corn being roughly pushed aside in a strange wave, and he could see the jagged saw-teeth of its path in the broken stalks. The formless panic leeched into his bones from the tiny organ that stored it. Whatever was cutting the drunken line was only an acre away from the yard.

Each step down the stairs rapped like a snare drum under his heels. He had brought the rifle around to his chest and the bayonet caught in the wood of the wall as he took the corner, making him spin and tumble the last few steps. By the time he made it to the kitchen he had removed the blade from his rifle and was repeatedly failing to sheath it. He tried to speak calmly but his voice came out high and choked.

"There's- something on- the way." The blade finally found its way home, but Declan noticed that he had cut his fingers twice in his panic.

Catherine pulled the griddle off the stove and set it on the table. In the same movement she cupped her hand around the mouth of the hurricane lamp and, with one quick puff, extinguished it, leaving them in the rotten pink glow of the moon.

"Holler if there's trouble." She grabbed the scatter gun and her heels knocked up the stairs.

Declan stayed low, looking through the broken window. His eyes adjusted, and all the while he thought everything moved in the darkness. Had the wind picked up? He heard, out in the yard, the weather crow creak.

The corn.

It was swaying, camouflaging any movement that might be happening within. Somewhere, infinitely far off it seemed, a shutter banged against something hollow and wooden. The pone smelled delicious as it cooled on the table.

Something crept from the corn.

It was a light grey shape, hunched down low and moving slowly, what must have been the head swinging back and forth like the lamp on a caboose.

Declan jerked the rifle to his shoulder. The barrel struck a shard of glass that still clung to the window. It shattered, and as bits of it tinkled onto the counter the face of the thing from the field flashed at him. It dashed off before he could get a shot, like a centipede from beneath a lifted rug. He backed from the window, rifle still up; hopping to the side to get a better angle, but the thing was out of sight.

"Oh, love... Oh, love..." He inhaled the first word, exhaled the last.

It had looked like there were spikes coming from out of its back. A pale, creeping porcupine.

Declan stood still, his mouth open wide to quiet his rapid breathing. He couldn't hear anything but the traitorous breeze and the ticking of the hidden clock. He counted the ticks; there was something wrong with the clock because they seemed to come with more and more space between them. His mouth dried out.

It was somewhere out there and he had to go out and find it.

He tried to recite Hail Mary under his breath as he made his way to the front room, but his tongue stuck to the top of his mouth. He saw nothing through the windows. He checked to make sure the chair was still firmly in place and crept back to the kitchen, shouldering the rifle and pulling the revolver. He unlocked the door and cautiously stepped out.

The breeze covered his footsteps as his boots crunched over the dry earth. He held the pistol before him and kept moving, making a slow circuit of the house. The barn door still seemed to be closed and latched, the front porch was bare, the only movement he caught was a furtive glimpse of Catherine peeking at him from her bedroom window.

Dry leaves began to scatter over the lawn as the strengthening wind tore them from the branches of the live oak in the yard. He could find no trace of the gray, spiny backed specter. Declan's eyes were beginning to throb from opening them so wide, as if they would let more light in.

He took another corner and his heart stopped for an instant. He caught sight of a hand in a window. It disappeared into the darkness of the interior and the drapery fell back into place. It hadn't been Catherine's hand. It was bloody and bandaged. He cocked the hammer on the revolver and knelt, crawling below the windows until he had reached the kitchen door. It was open and swinging in the wind. The revolver entered the house before he did.

A cloud had passed over the moon leaving the kind of darkness that his eyes could never get used to. The kitchen appeared to be empty. The far off knocking was louder inside, somehow. There were three gouges along the wall near the door to the front room. Declan moved painfully slowly to stay quiet. He tilted into the doorway.

It was in there, its back to Declan, the grey of it barely standing out against the dark curtains. Three spikes shooting from its back like a lopsided star-burst. Declan exhaled and fired.

It spun and roared, wild beard matted and dark. Something shone in its hand. Declan backed around the corner before the bullet shattered the doorjamb where he had just stood. The skills that had been beaten into him upon the anvil of war flared up in him coldly; he began to function like clockwork.

It was easier to fight when something was shooting back.

Unconsciously, the Colt was cocked and he swung around the jamb once more, aiming where the thing had been. He fired but the report was only answered by shattering glass. From behind the beaten couch the shade lifted into view and screamed. The muzzle of its gun flashed and Declan's arm was set ablaze before he could retreat to safety once more.

His back was flat against the wall, the fire on his arm made him breathe quickly. They can shoot? He hadn't seen a dead one handling a gun yet. It was quiet enough for him to hear Catherine's heel's slowly tokk-ing above. The situation didn't make sense. The dead never took cover like that.

"Aren't a dead man, are yah?" Declan called out.

"We're all dead men, brother. I just have a little more time on this earth than others." Replied a phlegmy voice.

"How's about we stop shootin' for a spell before we end up like, eh, them."

"Not sure if I can trust a man who'll shoot another man in the back."

Catherine's voice was punctuated by the snap of the hammers on her old scattergun.

"I've got a barrel for each of you if you don't quit shootin' up my house." She said calmly from the stairs.

"Yes, ma'am." Both men said.

* * *

The hour had grown late and the pone was a memory.

The big man had taken over the kitchen table with his collection of guns. After the altercation they had all gathered around the re-lit lamp and eaten, sharing their stories of the last few days. The newcomer's name was Hiram Coombs; he said he had been a Union Regular for the Illinois 101st regiment. The spikes Declan had seen turned out to be a cluster of rifles strapped to the man's back, which were now spread out on the table. Hiram was cleaning and reloading them with hands that didn't seem to need guidance. When he finished with each one he would hold it up and expound on its virtues.

He gave a carbine with a revolving chamber one last swipe with an oily rag.

"Colt, M1855; removed the safety and filed down the plate," He pointed at a small brass plate just behind the revolving bit that held the powder and lead.

"To stop back fire, chain fire, and *shit fire*." He roared with laughter, not unlike he had during the shootout. It was harrowingly loud and set Declan's hackles bristling. When Hiram saw that nobody joined in his laughter he slapped Declan on the back a little too hard.

"That's what we call a joke, son." His smile disappeared and he slung the carbine over his shoulder.

"Got to keep laughing; if you don't, you'll go mad."

He gave Declan the crazy eye and started taking apart a long rifle, the smile slowly returning to his face as he gazed at the glistening blue steel. One facet of the octagonal barrel threw back the lamp light.

"You haven't told us how you came here, nor have you given me a reason to let you take over my kitchen."

Catherine was scrubbing the skillet for the fifth time. The scatter-gun was between her and the sink. She hadn't sat down in an hour. The hammers on her gun were still cocked and it made Declan nervous.

"Ma'am, your hospitality is as warm as your smile." His lips grinned back at Catherine, but his eyes did not.

"I was on the firing line when those poor passed soldiers were raised up again. I saw, before my compatriots, that something was wrong. My keen eyes are known in three states."

"Known for what?" said Declan.

"Son, you need to learn to let a man finish his thoughts. I was saying I saw they were men no more, so I beat a cautious retreat, as any sane man would do in the circumstances." He looked at Declan and grinned. One canine was silver.

"Why, I believe *you* took to your heels before there was anything more fearsome than a campfire to run from." He winked.

"You didn't feel it. That dirty feeling on the wind. The emptiness of-"

"Can't say I have, son." Hiram broke in. He held up the rifle he had been cleaning.

"1863 Sharps. Ladder sight. Kill a man at five hundred yards and scare the devil out of him at a thousand. Falling block action removes the worry of fumbling with a percussion cap in the heat of a battle." This, too, went over his shoulder.

"How'd you afford all them fancy guns? If you were a rich lad, you'd be an officer." Declan spoke as he fiddled with his Navy revolver.

"Although I have always had an impeccable taste in firearms, if I may say so, I have not always had the means to purchase said pieces. Thus with the breakout of this most terrible scourge upon the land, I have had the distinct and irresolute height of gumption to partake in my fine collection, one that I hope will grow in these coming dark days."

"So, you've been stealing from the dead." said Declan, snapping his revolver shut, loaded and ready.

"One cannot steal from that which is dead, I think Aristotle said."

"Are you sure about that?"

"I am fairly certain that, you yourself, private, were not issued a fine revolver such as the Navy."

Declan frowned at the gun. "You're right."

There was a tense silence. The weather-cock screamed somewhere above. The wind was changing.

"I ask you... I heard a whinny from the barn as I was making my way though that blighted field of yours. As I am a man of honor, I will offer you two hundred American dollars, or its adjusted rate in Confederate currency, for your horse. Lady's choice."

Catherine stopped scrubbing. "Don't feel it's mine to offer."

"I'm not selling it to you." Declan had sheathed the pistol in his waistband, but immediately wished he had left it on the table.

"You are a canny businessman for an Irishman. I up my offer to two hundred fifty dollars, but not a penny more, for the rest of my funds will be going to my mother as soon as I can locate a post office. She is in desperate need of surgery on the retaining humors in her timorous. Dreadful condition. The surgeon told me, just before I left for the war, that if it wasn't taken care of it could spread to her solar plexus, which is already in a sorry state because of her rheumatism." It appeared as though a very real weight had been lowered onto his shoulders.

"That's a shame. If you start walking now you may make it to town by this time next week. Not sure if the post office still runs." Catherine said, flatly.

"You must love that horse dearly to turn down twice what it's worth and risk the life..." His eyes quickly scanned the two unbelieving bystanders and he broke off. His hands found the last gun on the table, a shotgun with a shattered stock.

"Tch! It sure is a shame that you took that cowardly shot at my back, son. This was a fine blunderbuss before you wrecked it." He held it closer to the lamp and picked the bullet out from the shards of wood.

"Say, ma'am? Do you suppose I could trouble you for a saw and plane so I can make a few quick adjustments to this-" He eyed Declan, "Once fine firearm?"

"There should be tools in the barn." Catherine was far away, staring out the window at something in the yard.

"That should do just fine. I'll just pop out there for a moment and freshen this old girl up a bit."

"I'm going with you." Declan was already on his feet, hand resting on the pistol.

Hiram chuckled lightly and smiled, tooth flashing.

"I understand son, you just want to see an artisan at work. How else are you going to learn, eh?"

He tilted the gun back over his shoulder, at ease.

"Shall we?" He gestured for Declan to lead the way.

"You can go on ahead, not sure if I remember the way." Declan nodded at the door.

"It is true, what they say," Hiram said, as Declan trailed him through the yard. "Some were meant to lead, and others to follow."

The clouds had cleared and the faint shadows of the men were longer than their souls.

"Listen, if you think for a *second* we believe you're anything but a cotton mouthed chiseler you can kick rocks."

"It's truly is a shame that you would have such mistrust in your fellow man. How will we defeat these fetid masses if we cannot trust each other?"

"You could start by givin' me a bit of the truth, now. What army do you fight for? The 101st regiment ain't been fightin' anywhere around here."

The door swung open, though Declan swore he had latched it. Ulysses could be heard bucking in the corner as they walked in.

"Of course I wasn't with the 101st when this abomination happened. I was providing special aid, on loan from Colonel..." Ulysses whinnied and backed into the shadows away from the new comer.

"Lawler?" Declan found and lit a lamp with a box of lucifers on the workbench. He went to Ulysses, who was cowering in the corner. It took a number of soothing sounds before the horse settled enough for him to place a calming hand upon it.

"Something's wrong, Ulysses is spooked."

"Yes, of course. General Wrathbone sent for me specifically, asking Colonel Lawler for the best marksman within five days ride. He was especially lucky; as I would hazard that there isn't a better shot within twenty days ride."

Declan smacked his lips with distaste. Hiram arranged the tools that were scattered about the workbench and clamped the injured shotgun in a leg vice.

"Hey, stay tight, I think there's somethin' foul about."

Declan looked at each corner of the barn, but they were too dark for the orange flicker of the lamp to penetrate.

"Yes, this will do just fine. You are going to be a whole new breed when I've finished with you, old girl."

"You talk like you've married the thing."

"She was my first love. Still is, I suppose. Had her for ten years now. She's grown with me."

Hiram grabbed a short wood-saw and, with a pained look on his face, began sawing off the stock just before it began to splinter from the bullet.

"I've modified her workings over the years. The trigger is so light a mosquito could trip it with the breeze of its wing, a baby could pull back the hammer, you could shoot it every five minutes for a week and come away without a blister."

The damaged wood fell away, leaving an angular protuberance six inches behind the trigger.

"She can fire paper cartridges with a cap or those fancy new copper jackets with the cap built in."

Hiram began shaping an angular jut in what was left of the stock with a curved blade meant to trim horse hooves. Soon it looked like a rounded pistol grip.

Declan left him to his work and, while still keeping an eye on the big man, soothed the uneasiness out of Ulysses again. He offered the horse some pemmican, but it wouldn't take it.

"There you are, Colette, a fancy new grip. Let's see how you handle."

Hiram released the gun from the vice and began to swing it around. Declan pulled his revolver and had it aimed by the second swing.

"Settle your flock, son. She isn't loaded. Just need to feel her out."

Hiram continued to pull ridiculous poses, aiming at odd angles and grunting each time. Declan returned the pistol to his belt, but kept narrowed eyes on Hiram. Ulysses grunted.

"Poor girl's top heavy. I'm going to have to give you a little trim-"

He broke off, both men glanced about quickly. There had been a hollow knocking coming from the direction of the house, the same sound Declan had heard earlier.

"No mind, a shutter in the wind." Declan said.

"My stars." Hiram ran his fingernails through his scalp. "Aren't we all."

The shotgun was once again clamped. Hiram snatched a sharp edged bastard file from the array of tools and made a marking cut ten inches down from the muzzle.

"I'm sorry girl, I'm afraid you will never take a grouse down at fifty yards again. I'll make it quick."

He feverishly began sawing, his frown at a pinnacle on the push stroke.

"All-most-all-most-there-there-there...ah!" The scream of the file ceased and the larger part of the barrel dropped to the dirt floor. There was a smell of hot metal.

"I do declare, it would appear you've lost a couple pounds, darling." He grabbed a finer file and began taking the rough edges off of the new barrel.

"So smooth, so lithe."

"Have you ever had a, eh, lady friend, Hiram?" Declan was watching the harsh strokes of the file, stroking the horses mane faster and faster, until he caught himself, blushed, and gave Ulysses a couple stern slaps on the flank.

"Legion were their name, there is nothing in this world filled with more lies and sin than a woman. But a good rifle..." He gave one long, slow, stroke with the file.

"A rifle will treat you as well as you treat it. Only a fool would expect anything close to that from a person. Man or woman."

"I don't know about that, there's good folk out there..."

"There, isn't that beautiful?" Hiram said as he turned around, the gun balanced on his index finger. With the pistol grip and the short barrel it looked more like a gargantuan pistol than a rifle. He slipped a finger into one of the many pouches on his belt and pulled out a paper cartridge. He carefully thumbed it into the open breech. "I fear that in the coming dark days Collette is going to be put to work more often than I'd like."

"We've left Catherine alone too long." Declan said. "If you're done feelin' up that gun we should get a move on."

"Christ, you Irish have no passion." Said Hiram, sliding the gun over his back.

"We try to love things that can love us back."

"Maybe you just don't realize that true love does not exist, my young friend. That the more trust you put into a person, the more they will use you to their own ends. Whatever love you have felt was just a person keeping you happy while they used you."

Declan's face went slack and pale. He took a step back.

"Hah!" Hiram was checking every little mechanism in the shotgun. "Is that some sort of shock to you? I suppose I was your age when I figured out this grand truth. Probably a little bit younger."

"Watch yourself." Declan breathed, drawing his pistol.

"Oh! Did I touch upon a sore nerve? Does the truth hurt?" Hiram held the shotgun defensively.

"Get down, *idjit*." Declan held the Navy in steady aim.

"Son, you're going to have to speak up if you want to give orders, pistol or no." Hiram slowly sank to his knees, grinning mockingly.

Declan took aim and fired.

"Christ!"

The dead one that had crept up behind Hiram took the bullet in the shoulder with a shrug. It howled and grabbed the big man's neck just as he flinched. Hiram choked, eyes wide with surprise. He ineffectually elbowed the dead man in the ribs. Declan swore as he walked to the skirmish. He put the barrel of the pistol to the corpse's temple and pulled the trigger.

*Click.*

The dead one flung Hiram's body around and knocked Declan off balance, onto his ass. The ghouls stained teeth closed around Hiram's ear. His windpipe was squeezed so tight, Hiram could only make a phlegmy wheezing noise.

Declan breathed deep. Took aim. Fired once more.

*Click.*

Hiram's tongue was dangling from his mouth like that of a hanged man.

"Guck." He uttered, eyes rolling back and going milky white.

Declan rose to his feet. Swore an oath, and pulled the bayonet.

"Enough'a this."

He took three fast steps forward and stabbed the abomination through its neck just as it was biting into the meat surrounding Hiram's neck.

The thing let out a shriek that could only be compared to a dozen frogs stuck on a jack-knife. Declan pulled the blade back and opened another sucking wound in its neck, down by the shoulder.

It released and fell back, shuddering until the spirit left it.

Hiram felt about his neck where the hands had choked him. He sucked in air and tumbled onto his side, gasping breaths puffing clouds of dust.

Declan pulled him to his feet. The big man collected his shotgun. He rubbed his wounded ear sheepishly.

"I am a *humble* man..."

"Don't even say anything." Declan worried over the works of the pistol. "Let's get back to Catherine."

They walked back to the house in silence, both of them eying the corn as though it were a living, dangerous thing.

The lamp was out in the kitchen when they went around back, and Catherine was nowhere to be seen. Everything was as they had left it, just as dark and lonely. Declan began to call for Catherine, but was hushed immediately.

"Shh!" Hiram hissed. "You can get yourself killed when I'm not around, thanks much." He pulled two shining revolvers that had been concealed in his coat.

"Corpus Christi, you must weigh three hundred pounds with all them guns." Declan whispered.

"It makes for good exercise."

"It makes for a hunchback."

"The same could be said of your mother."

Before Declan could retaliate, Hiram had already winked and crept into the front room. It was as empty as the kitchen. The wind caught a crack in one of the windows and it whistled like a man looking down into a very deep hole. A floorboard creaked upstairs and they froze for a moment, staring at each other. The sound did not recur, so they pressed on. Declan frowned when Hiram motioned for him to go up the stairs first, but he relented.

His pistol was drawn and ready. It was pitch black upstairs. All of the doors were closed. They heard a snap from Catherine's room and headed that way, ignoring the other doors. It was unlocked.

For a moment, Declan faced down the twin abysses of a scatter-gun. Hiram squeaked and ducked. The only word that came to Declan's lips was *Mother*. The gun swung away and the silver gauze of Catherine's hair replaced it.

"Christ, don't sneak up on me. I could've dropped dead. Come, *see...*" She grabbed Declan by the sleeve and pulled him to the window.

"They're in the corn."

Declan took in the view. He coughed and stepped back. He looked up to the dark ceiling and his lips moved, though he saw nothing up there and he didn't say a thing. Hiram pushed past him and Declan tripped on the rug, sitting down hard on the straw of Catherine's bed. Hiram blocked half the light of the window as he cursed what he saw through it. The light dimmed further as though the whole house were sinking below ground. The clouds had shifted with the angry wind, and they had brought the rain along with them.

Declan remembered the one good day he'd ever had with his father. He'd been shaken out of his bed before sunrise. His father smelled different because he hadn't taken a drink yet.

It was spring and they were going fishing. The family had been nearly starving for a month and his father planned a trip to a lake far in the wilderness that had hardly been touched. He rode with his father on a horse named Spud for over two hours through barely beaten wilderness. They didn't speak during the ride, his father murmured prayer the entire way, stopping only to point out random bits of nature and to say, "Look lad, a *sign*."

When they finally reached the lake, Declan jumped down from the lumpy saddle and ran to the water. His father scolded him, saying that he was scaring the fish. Declan didn't stop. He was so thankful to be off the lame lumpy horse and at his goal.

He splashed the clean distant water on his face and it felt so good he hardly even felt his father's palm smacking the back of his head.

They fished all afternoon. The First hour they caught nothing but it seemed just as they were about to give up his father's line got a bite. His father reeled it in, and it was a five pounder. After that, the huge lazy fish of the hidden pond seemed to be whipped into a frenzy by the presence of the outsider's exotic night-crawlers. As soon as the bait would hit the water, the crystal surface would ripple with the legion of bass, longing to be dragged up into the unknown.

That is what took Declan's breath away when he beheld the field. The way it churned and waved with hungry activity. The fish were out there. The three of them were the bait. To try and count the number of things moving in the field would have been trying to count the stars in the sky.

"This house is far from a fortress, ma'am." Hiram said, without taking his eyes from the window. "It seems it would be prudent to flee."

"Run if you want, boys," Catherine straightened up nearly as tall as Hiram, her back popping audibly. "I ain't goin' nowhere."

Hiram sighed and aggressively scratched at the back of his shaggy head. "I'll offer you three hundred dollars for the horse; you owe it to the beast, it will only be torn to shreds by those monsters if it stays here with you suicidal fools."

"The horse isn't for sale. You can take to your heels." Declan stood firm with his hand resting on the butt of the revolver. He tried to remember if he had reloaded it. "We don't need you."

Hiram breathed loudly through his nose.

"Very well, I shall leave you to your fate. I wish you the best of luck." His eyes said the opposite. He received no response from the two but a stare. He stomped out the door, his guns thumping against the frame. The two were silent while they listened to the big man pounding down the stairs.

"He's going to steal the horse." said Catherine.

Declan examined the revolver. It was loaded, but a small sliver of wood had gotten wedged near the firing pin. He swore and picked it out as he went to the window. Hiram was headed right for the barn.

She joined him at the window. Hiram was standing at the barn door, staring down at the latch with his arms crossed. His head perked up like a startled deer and he jogged out of view of the window.

"Something wasn't right about him." Declan grabbed his pack and shouldered it. "Didn't talk right for an enlisted man. We've got to get somewhere safer than this. There's too many windows."

"I could lock you in the cellar, if you please." She replied, dry as leaves. There was a lightness in her voice, betraying a few too many drops from the purple bottle.

"Christ, woman, we've got scores of them awful things comin' this way. I reckon we have half an hour before that fog gets here." Declan waited for a moment and brought his rifle off his shoulder. Her face was as hard as slate. It could cut.

"Catherine, I need your help. There's no way I can do this on my own. With you I might have a chance at makin' it to mornin'. Now, I know you wanna die, but I surely don't."

Catherine turned and looked through the broken window. The grave looked like it was heaving gently as the waving corn cut the moonlight to ribbons. The fog took up most of the sky.

"I suppose you wouldn't."

"Will you help me?" Declan put his hand on her shoulder.

"Fine." She turned to him and spit in her hand. "But promise me, if you're alive in the morning, you'll get the hell out of here and leave me be."

Declan looked down at her glistening palm and laughed. He spat into his own.

"Only if you're with me."

She pulled her hand back for a moment then shook her head and took his hand. Her grip was surprisingly firm.

"Fine. You'd best not bother me in hell."

"Perish the thought."

* * *

They locked and barred the doors. All the furniture they could move was crammed before the fragile windows. The few supplies they had were moved upstairs to Catherine's room. Catherine staked out the window there while Declan stood in the kitchen, hovering over the small gap in the barricaded window.

All too soon there was movement. The gap was too small to see any more than a slice of the field. He swore and tore the barricade away from the broken window. They had done too good of a job sealing themselves off. The rain was spattering down, sounding like a rushing river beating down on the corn leaves.

The field was alive. The dead were in the yard. The rainclouds had poured ink over the landscape, the only highlights were the white shines of wetness on the dead men. They crawled from the corn like rats escaping a flood. He fired on the nearest one, which screamed and ran for the window. His second shot took its head off. As soon as it fell, one of its brothers dove upon it and began tearing the corpse with its teeth.

Declan counted six when he first cleared the window. Already there were eight. This group seemed slower, more deteriorated, like they had lain for a number of days before they had risen. Two of them were missing limbs and crawling through the increasingly muddy dirt of the yard. There was a boom from above and the closest one was shoved writhing to its back. When it tried to push itself back up, Declan scored a shot to its neck and it fell back, motionless.

"That's one for me!" Catherine shouted from above.

"Half of one, I finished it off. Wait until they get closer with that scatter-gun."

"Pfui!"

More were emerging; he fired four more times with careful aim and four more dropped.

A dozen replaced them.

The real panic finally flowed when Declan set to reloading his rifle. He had enough bullets to reload five more times. He knew there were far more dead out there than he could shoot. Hiram didn't seem like such a fool any more. Declan wished he himself was weighed down with rifles and ammo.

He slipped into a killing flow for a dozen more shots, firing, fanning the lever action, reloading. Some fell with a single shot, others two. A huge lumbering bear of a man took three bullets and a blast from Catherine's scatter-gun before it fell, just short of the porch. One came screaming from the field, a fancy looking officer that ran like a sprinter. Declan fired twice and the thing tumbled onto the porch, still shaking with idiot rage, grasping at the new craters in its back.

"Christ-" Declan shook his head and shouldered his rifle. If he kept up his current plan he would be out of ammo in another five minutes. There were too many, and they were too close. So many empty eyes and hungry mouths. The distant lightning that illuminated the yard did nothing but enhance each horrible twist and mortal stain.

The field was nothing but hazy pink. The tendrils of fog tumbled from the corn and out onto the lawn. Declan was certain he saw the grave heave before he wedged the table back in front of the window. He ran upstairs.

"Oh, love. Oh, love."

"What are you doing? They've gotten to the porch!" Catherine shouted over her shoulder.

"This ain't working. Not enough bullets. Too many." He caught his breath. "If we can lock up in the barn, there's no windows there."

Glass shattered downstairs and the furniture they had worked to block themselves in was thundering to the floor. Moans curdled up the walls and found them upstairs.

Declan ran to the window. There were about twenty in the yard, some stumbling mindlessly in the mud, others taking advantage of their fallen fellows, tearing them apart, never seeming to get their fill. A few others crouched in the dark places of the yard, gazing about with a terrible canniness. Declan took one of these down, then reloaded. Footsteps clambered up the stairs. Catherine closed and locked the door before the foul things came into sight.

"We'd be better off in the barn. You got good legs?"

"What kind of question is that?"

I'm gonna clear a path, then we jump down off the roof and run, yeah?"

"That's crazy. I could but I won't."

The door began shuddering on its hinges. It didn't sound very strong. Declan reached to grab her.

"I'm not gonna let you die-" His hand never touched her. She had wedged the gun under his chin.

"Don't you touch me you goddamn *murderer*." she hissed.

Declan slapped the gun aside and turned away in disgust.

He grabbed her bed and slid it in front of the door.

"I'm done with you, ma'am." He opened the window all the way and climbed out to the roof of the porch.

He stepped carefully, as it was slick with the rain that continued to thrush down. Now that he was outside he could see the fearful panorama of twisted souls jerking through the cold pink mist. Most of them were torn up badly, moving as though the mist were water.

If there weren't many fast ones he would have a chance at making it to the barn. The mist and the rain worked together to hide anything past a handful of yards, the barn barely peeking out of the haze. He glanced over his shoulder at the window one last time before he jumped, but Catherine had drawn the curtains. He sighed and made sure the bayonet held fast.

He crossed himself and jumped.

The soggy earth caught him softly and he was running as soon as he landed. He leaped over a dead one that lay crippled in the mud. It reached out impotently as Declan passed, but the only thing that touched him was the stink. Yards later, a dead one stumbled into Declan's path that he could not avoid. He slowed and leveled the rifle, fired. The bullet punched a terrible hole in its chest, but on it marched. Declan grunted and lashed out with the bayonet, tearing the thing's neck open and shoved it to the side. He'd run past by the time the wound began to ooze slow, dead blood. He dodged two more before he finally made it to the barn.

The door was ajar, making Declan immediately suspicious. He didn't have any time to puzzle over it. Two screaming purple streaks came screaming from the mist, their naked bodies covered in cuts and bruises. He slid into the dark barn and slammed the heavy latch into place.

The two outside immediately began thrashing on the door, making it shiver on its hinges. Their racket was more than Declan could bare. An overwrought madness took him over and he began screaming at the door, as though he could fight them with noise alone. Something caught in his throat and he doubled over in a coughing fit. By the time he caught his breath he had also regained his composure.

Declan could hardly see anything, the only light being a few weak razors that filtered down through the boards above in the hayloft. He couldn't hear Ulysses.

"Ulysses, boy-" He called above the growing racket, it sounded like there were more outside banging on the door.

"Are yah still with us?" He shouldered his rifle and stepped slowly forward. There was a snort in the dark.

"Ah, there you are, thank the Lord you're alright."

Declan's foot kicked something that scraped over the ground. He bent and picked up the broken handled spade he had dropped earlier.

"That *is* you, isn't it?" He choked up on the handle and felt the weight. The graceful curving edge was sharp and serrated from rough use.

"Hope I didn't scare you with all the screamin'." He whispered.

His eyes had adjusted slightly but he could only make out the rough outlines of his surroundings. The wheels of the cart, the work bench, doors to the stalls. Declan barely heard a scuffle from the farthest stall and moved around the cart cautiously. It was in the darkest corner of the barn, and might as well have been painted black. The door was partly open, too dark to see anything past it. The spade was tight in his hands as he drew it back to ready. He nudged the stall door the rest of the way open with his boot.

There was a scream from within the stall and the world swung upward until the side of Declan's head stopped it. He had lost his footing as though someone had pulled a rug out from underneath him. Unseen hands had latched onto his ankles. He was sliding in the dirt toward the cart; his feet disappeared into the blackness beneath. He kicked at his attacker frantically but it would not let go. The slats of light above were blocked out by a silhouette that swooped down from the dark stall he had just opened. In a blink it was all he could see.

Just before the living shadow set upon him, Declan dug the edge of the spade into the dirt and levered the sharp point of the broken handle up into its path. The handle slid into the things dark flesh and it rolled off to the side, squealing like a stuck pig.

*"Danny! Danny, why'd you leave me to them?"* It gurgled as it rolled and flopped. Declan could see its shape and the shine of wet blood on its neck.

*"Why, Danny?"*

He yanked the short spade back before the thing could writhe away. Mercilessly, he stabbed about his feet at his other attacker, in no way sure he was even landing any blows in his fury.

It sounded like there were a thousand demon drummers at the door. The horrible wet thing twisted and howled on the floor next to him and he still couldn't see a damn thing. He screamed, each time he plunged the point into the void beneath the wagon.

"Why! Why! *Why!*"

He had gotten tangled in an old fishing line once after diving into a swimming hole. He was only able to break free just before his lungs burst and he gulped in the lake. That is what it felt like to him just now, but it was taking much longer. His lungs had burst and he could only scream, knowing no one would hear him.

The handle must have struck something tender to the dead one because the grip finally released. Declan scrambled back, the dirt he kicked up got in his eyes. He spun his legs from beneath the wagon, rose to his knees and let the sharp edge of the spade fall on the still thrashing shape beside him until it lay still.

He breathed hard, raspy breaths, head twisting; looking for something, anything. He knew there was at least one dead one left in the barn, even more maybe. The barn door was making frightful cracking noises, bending before the weight of the dead. He gave the wagon wide berth as he circled it, treading back to the center of the barn. He forced himself to slow and focus, blinking the dirt from his eyes as he tried to remember where the ladder to the hayloft was. After only two steps towards the ladder he heard something snap to his right. He swung at the sound, cutting nothing but the air between him and the unknown.

With his free hand waving before him, he eventually found the comforting smoothness of the well-worn ladder. He slipped the shovel between two of his belt loops and began climbing. Halfway up a searing pain burned up his leg. The dead one had snuck up and gotten a hold on his leg, sinking its teeth into his boot, squeezing tendons and pinching the flesh.

Declan yelped as he was pulled down a rung. It pulled harder. He felt his grip loosening. He was pulled down another step. He stopped any further descent by hooking an arm over a rung. The thing's terrible clawed hand was scratching at his thigh. With his free hand he grabbed the pistol from his waistband and fired at his feet.

The scratching stopped; he heard it fall back, howling. Declan clambered the rest of the way up, doing his best to ignore the phantom teeth in his ankle.

The barn door cracked as he reached the top and a vibrating slice of light played over the dirt floor when he looked back.

The hayloft was a shade brighter than below. Declan could feel a bit of the madness that had settled on him abating, now that his eyes could focus on something asides from darkness. He dodged the few moldy bales that remained and made his way to the open door at the head of the loft.

Outside, insanity awaited him. Below, he could see a half dozen of the dead attacking the barn door. He was sure it wouldn't stand up to much more with how it bent and cracked. The yard was briefly lit by a flash of lightning. Catherine knelt on the roof of the porch. She fired into her window. It exploded and glass rained down onto the shingles. The wind pulled out the drapes and they flapped, waving like arms out of the jagged opening. Then, bloodied arms truly did reach out at Catherine, who had cocked the second barrel, waiting for the right moment. He shouted to her.

"Catherine!"

The yard between them was clear, save for the clutch of dead at the barn door. The rest of the mob had either moved on or swarmed into the house. Declan couldn't tell.

"Fancy seeing you! Thought you ran away."

"The horse is gone; you should join me in the cellar if you decided on livin'."

"Still want to die, just not like *this*."

"Fine! Get to the cellar; I'll take care of these."

She didn't respond, but fired her final round into the window. Dropping the shotgun, she started carefully climbing down from the roof.

Above the loft door was a pulley for lifting hay-bales. He found a length of rope coiled beside him and threaded it through the pulley. Taking the other end with him, he made his way to the back of the loft and tied the rope soundly around the largest bale he could find. There was a great shuddering crack below as Declan passed the ladder. He stopped, bending to see if the door had given way.

A hand shot through the opening, grabbed him by the throat and pulled him down to lie flat on the floor.

The thing was breathing cold stinking gurgles into his face, blood spurting from the fresh wound on its neck. Declan braced himself with one hand to keep from falling and reached back with his free hand to snap the bayonet from his rifle. He slammed the blade down and it slid into the horror's eye socket.

Gore sprayed up at Declan with two fat pulses and the thing released him, tumbling down into the darkness where his brethren were already gathering with hungry jaws. It took the blade with it. Declan could see it glinting as the dead ones swarmed like ants on a fallen starling.

Declan scrambled back over the bales, coughing and gagging. The mist had grown thicker, but the yard appeared to be clear. Catherine stood half concealed by the cellar, glancing left and right like a hunted prairie dog. He swung out on the rope and began lowering himself down like he had at basic training. He'd gone a few feet before he heard Catherine's shouts of warning.

While he had been focusing on climbing, one of the horrors had come back out of the barn. Declan's feet dangled just a foot over its reaching hands. It grabbed the rope and pulled, snapping it like a whip.

Declan could do little to control the spin he was sent into, and although his grip held true, he felt himself descend. He fought the urge to vomit and wrestled the pistol from his waistband.

He fired twice, but missed woefully. The rope was coiling in the dirt as he was tugged closer. He fired once more and the crown of its head split, the contents spilling through its mouth and painting a shape in the dirt that reminded him of Missouri.

Declan groaned. Another of the dead had emerged from the barn. It picked up where the other had left off. The spinning was getting to him.

He could no longer keep track of anything as the world turned liquid and swirled about him. He fired twice more until the revolver snapped empty.

He put it away and looked up, trying to relieve his nausea, only to see the yellow brown blur of the hay bale above him, under the pulley. All of the pulling had dragged it from the loft, and now it hung ponderously above him. He forced one last hard spin around the rope and let go, flying down ten feet and landing wrong on his heels, pitching him back, sitting down hard.

He tried to stand up, but his swinging head told him to roll over and over like a drunk. After his second attempt to stand, he was able to focus long enough to see the dead one release the rope. A blink later the yellow smear of the bale streaked down and the thing folded beneath it with a dozen syncopated crunches. A hand still protruded from beneath the bale, reaching toward Declan even as the body it belonged to died.

He laid down. The cold, wet, dirt felt good on the back of his head; it helped the world slow down. He felt the hot barrel of the pistol burning his hip bone where he had thrust it in his waistband, but he did not act to move it. He was tired all of a sudden, the little bones in his back felt tight and hot, so he didn't see much sense in moving them from the soothing earth. Someone was calling to him, but when he tried to respond he had to turn his head and vomit into the mud. It made him feel a little better. He left his mouth open and let the cool rain fall on his boiling tongue.

Catherine was kicking him in the ribs.

"Git up you lazy mick! If you're gonna be such an insufferable ass about letting me die, so can I!"

"Esh, mother, I might get up if you stop kickin' me."

She helped pull him to his feet while continuing to berate him. He stumbled after her, barely keeping his feet as they crossed the yard. Declan looked over to the cornfield before they made it to the cellar door. The grave mound was disturbed, mud thrown left and right of it as though something had burst out.

Declan tried not to think about what that meant and certainly didn't say anything about it, as Catherine didn't seem to notice.

He got dizzy on the stairs and tumbled down past Catherine and into the dust. He stayed on his back as she swung the angled doors closed and latched it above them. He heard her heels carefully grind down the flagstone steps. She kicked him lightly in the side.

"Get up. You got a lucifer? I got a lamp down here somewhere."

Declan sat up and felt the wetness at the back of his head. He couldn't be sure if it was blood or even if it was his. He rifled through his pockets and handed her his match safe. He heard its screw top chirp open and bits of lightning flicked, burning his eyes till a gentle flame left Catherine's face gently illuminated.

"A grand plan you had-" she said, cut off by a booming strike to the door that somehow was not muffled by the clay of the walls. The match dropped and she lit another. Declan rolled to his knees and pushed himself up. He watched as the match floated from shelf to shelf along the wall until it passed a hurricane lamp that glowed brown with dust when she lit it.

"What now?" she said, "Do we wait for hell to bust in here and take us, or do we take that damn fool shovel of yours and dig down there ourselves?"

Declan found he could balance on his feet, though he didn't like it.

The cellar was like any number he had seen before. Dirt walls surrounding dust laden shelves, sprinkled with jars of preserves.

There was an egg crate in the corner that held a number of religious relics. They bore no dust.

"We're gonna be fine, mother. We should've come down here in the first place, like we was waitin' out a storm."

"Declan, I don't think this storm is gonna pass." She grabbed a jar from the shelf, wiped off the dust, and handed it to him.

"Here, a boy has to eat. Shame to die hungry."

Declan twisted the ring of the lid till it snicked open and a briny garlic spirit filled the air. He plucked a fat pickle from it and crunched down. He had been living off of bland food for so long the tartness shocked his cheeks. He spoke, mouth half full.

"We ain't gonna die, ma'am. We wait this out till mornin', make a run for it. Most of 'em are slow; we can dodge 'em easy if we can see 'em."

"You know as well as I those filthy things are gonna bust down that door and tear us up like foxes in a hen house."

"Not gonna let that happen, ma'am."

The pounding on the door suddenly doubled up, causing Declan to jump. He finished the pickle, wiped his fingers, and started reloading. Catherine set the lamp down and sat in a dark corner.

"Should've pulled the trigger before you showed up. I shouldn've seen all this."

"Keep on with that talk and I'll plug you here and now, mother."

She stamped her foot, raising an umber cloud.

"That's fine! Do it! A favor for both of us. The only thing I have to look forward to is a drop of laudanum, and I'm running terrible low. If we live through this night I'll be hungry tomorrow and hungry that night. I'll be hot or cold or wet or lost. It ain't never gonna end. Why? I don't even have the house any more. I can't fix all this. It was one thing when it was just me that was broken, but now *everything* is." She grabbed the crate of relics and dashed it against the wall with a crash.

"What moon-eyed thing you got to say to that?" She was breathing hard, tears in her eyes.

"There's always somethin' ma'am. Livin' hurts, yeah, but, I don't know- I'm so young. I feel like an edjit tellin' you. I can't remember the last time I had an easy day or a toe that wasn't blistered. I got two no-good brothers and a dead mother. I'm a deserter and a coward. I can just hope things get better if I keep moving. Things have to get better than this."

Doom.

"There's so much I haven't done." His voice was cracking. "Corpus Christi, I've killed a dozen men in this war and-" He looked down intently at the oiled works of his rifle. "And I haven't even known the touch of a woman." He sniffed and wiped quickly at his eye.

Doom.

The fury drained from Catherine's face and was replaced with motherly compassion. She went to him and hugged him, his head finding the comforting nook of her neck, the cold rifle pinned between them.

"You poor pup. You weren't made for all this." They swayed for a moment like they were moved by a gentle tide.

Doom.

He pulled away from her and turned to the doors.

Doom.

"It won't be long now."

Doom.

He handed her the revolver.

"Here, hold off using this until, em, until you have to."

He looked over his rifle and pointed it to the door, then thought better of it and grabbed the shovel from his belt.

Doom.

"It won't be-"

A hand, twisted and broken by the force, burst through a board of the half rotten door. Declan lashed out, screaming.

"Not us! Not now!" He came down on the flopping hand with the sharp edge of the spade. The crooked thing dropped from the wrist like an overripe apple from its branch.

"Ha!" He was mad at the sight.

The stump pulled back and was instantly replaced with another grasping, hungry hand. Declan remedied it in a similar manner. Gore sprayed the dusty steps.

There was a wild look in Declan's eye, the sort one could see in a hunter that kept shooting when he had bagged more than he could carry.

"God!" He lashed out.

"*Why?*" Three fingers were cleft from a groping hand. The digits wriggled on the ground like some disgusting bait a ghoul would dig up.

"Why here, huh?" He chopped again. "Why *now?*" He took the broad side of the spade down on the wriggling fingers like a smithy's sledge. "Things weren't hard enough, were they?"

A dead hand pulled back at a board of the door and it gave way with a crack like a gunshot. Everything was sounding explosive to Declan. The rage that rushed through his veins, his tendons, his tight racing heart, amplified everything.

Three arms searched for him now, and he could see the waning lamp glow in their hungry empty eyes.

"Lamps almost dead." His flushed ears heard Catherine murmur.

"*Grand!*" He lopped another wrist with the ragged edge of the spade.

The blood that collected on the stairs, thick and thin, was diluted by the sour tasting rain that washed over the walking corpses and down through the crack they'd created. As Declan chopped at each crop of arms the muddy slurry of fluids coursed down the steps and came to curdle in a coppery smelling puddle at a low-point in the cellar. Catherine watched it grow in the dying lamp light, as everything else she could see were only moving shadows that she could no longer interpret. She tapped the revolver to her temple to remind herself that both it and she still existed. The blood was all she could see.

The lamp went out with three flickers and no fade.

"Father!" Chop. "Son!" Chop. "*Holy ghost!*" Chop.

Another board gave way.

There was room for one more. Declan took a step back to allow for the pile of gore that was accumulating at the door. All he could see was the choked moonlight playing on the hands.

Declan flailed, whatever demon was in him had taken physical pain from him and turned it into pure hate.

Despite the dead tide that broke over him, Declan's fevered mind forced the memory on him of the last time he had felt the way he did.

Turned into this mindless chopper and extinguisher of the cancerous and adipose.

His mind wandered. The clockwork of his body disposed of the dirty work.

* * *

"Doc says there's nothin' he can do."

"Doubt there's anything the Lord Jesus could do; way you treated the corpus, Dah."

"Damn whelp, all I can do is drink the dirty water an' piss blood an' this is all I get from yah?"

"You'd led a clean life, maybe you'd be pissin' water and be surrounded by loved ones, but that's not the path you chosen. issit?"

The elder's face twisted with the kind of pain thumbscrews usually caused.

"Did nothin' but toil an' give for ya, boy. Two sons, I could'a handled."

The father, younger than he looked, reached beneath his pillow and retrieved a flask.

"*You're* the one tha' drove me to drink."

He took a long slow swig.

Declan's fist tensed and a knuckle popped tight by his side.

"Mah said you did plenty of that before I came along."

"Yer mahs an idjit an' a liar." He sneered and took another sip. "Don't even know if yer mine. Don't look a damn thing like me."

Declan was shaking.

"You know damn well we're blood, Dah. We got the same birthmark."

The old man's eyes bulged; he stifled his laughter with the bottle, which was soon empty.

"Gave you that mark when you were wee. Used my buck knife! Hell of a lark, yeah?"

Declan's hands were kneading the air like bread dough. He grabbed a spare pillow and squeezed it instead.

"You, you son of a bitch. Any wrong I done to you in bein' born I repaid *three-fold*." Declan was gasping, he'd never spoken this plainly to the statue that was his father and each word was a millstone across his tongue.

"I tried so hard to make you happy, dah."

The elder's head was nodding. He let the flask tumble to the floor with a clank. There was a tiny drop of the amber dew on his mustache. His face looked heavy, eyes drooping.

"Could'na tried too hard, ain't been happy since you..."

He drifted off and began snoring high in his nose. Declan stifled a whimper with a sniff and a clearing of the throat. The pillow was still choking in his hands. He shuffled, quaking and numb, to his father's side. He took one choppy breath and stuffed the pillow over the old man's face.

His father burst into a short lived frenzy, his weakened state reduced what would have once been right hooks and hay-makers to baby slaps. Declan frowned down with scared eyes, his mind trying to understand what his body was doing. His arms pressed down harder, his father's movements were growing weaker. It would only last a few more moments.

\* \* \*

A sallow nail grazed his cheek, bringing his mind back to his body. Arms like torches, lungs like bellows, with the in and out, no idea as to how long he had been felling the flesh. He took another careful move back on the slippery stairs. The right half of the door had been torn wide. There was no way he and his stumpy shovel could do this work any longer.

"Holdin' the fort there, mother?" He called out into the darkness behind him. Something, a jar probably, crashed and tinkled to the ground. He stopped chopping for a moment when a new sound arose from behind the horde that clogged the door. It rose up above the flat hum of groans, in the way a badly struck violin note could ring through an entire brass section. He shuddered at what the sound meant and redoubled his bloody work, hoping he could drown it out before Catherine could hear it. It was the piercing squeal of a madwoman's voice, screeching:

"Mother! Mother! Why can't you help us?"

Declan began to sing the Lord's Prayer at the top of his lungs. The approach of the dead was slightly slowed by the wall of the fallen that had piled before the door.

"*Catherine*, are yah with me?"

He jabbed the point of the spade into the neck of a portly Confederate that had made its way over the charnel heap, twisting the blade just in time to keep the gore from channeling down all over him. He changed his footing and nearly slipped. Catherine didn't respond and when he looked over his shoulder he could see nothing past the bottom stair. The fat soldier stood gurgling, still reaching for Declan. Declan wound up and sank half of the blade deep into its thick neck, feeling the grisly click as it split vertebrae. It slumped, twitching, on top of the pile.

Declan swept his boot left and right over the step before him, clearing as much of the carnage as possible. His nose hurt, hardened from the hundred stinks slashing at his sinuses. Just as he had nearly forgotten it, the horrible voice of the dead woman returned in the lull. It was joined by a noise infinitely more disturbing than even the banshee wail had been.

The whole world stood still, even the impatient rain waited churning in the air. The only sound to break the eternal moment was the mewling cry of the sickest, hungriest infant Declan had ever heard. There was nothing he could do to drown it out, he was sick to his marrow just imagining the horrible little lump that was making the noise. It rose and rose, even when time started moving again, even when the onslaught redoubled and there were four sets of arms clambering over the corpse wall for them.

He backed down the last two steps swinging wildly and bent to pick up his rifle. It had been in the path of the bloody runoff and was covered in it. He feverishly rubbed the works with his jacket, hoping and praying it would still fire.

"Catherine! Mother!" He gasped, not daring to turn his back on the dead. "I need you *now*!"

There was a gentle pressure on the back of his neck. He barely heard the slick oiled click of the revolver's hammer over the cacophony. His lungs stopped like he had been dunked under ice water. Catherine whispered into his ear.

"We weren't meant for this world, son."

There was a pistol shot.

The dead did not seem to notice.

## CHAPTER 17

Hiram cursed when the horse lost its footing. The rain was getting harder and the path was turning to a treacherous slurry of mud. The horse's hooves sank deeper and deeper under the heavy weight of Hiram and the artillery strapped to his back.

They had traveled only a handful of miles in the last half hour. Hiram questioned stealing the beast in the first place.

He hoped that when he finally reached a town that there would be a telltale flag hanging from a porch to let him know which side was in favor. His current outfit would get him shot in the proper company. He had been lucky to stumble upon the strange pair at the house and not a militant farmer.

The oilcloth he had draped over his weaponry came loose and began to flap in the wind like an ugly cape. He reached painfully behind himself and grabbed the loose corner to tie it down again. The horse whinnied and began to turn defiantly back the way they had come.

"Horse," Said Hiram, as he secured the oilcloth. "I've spared you the spur thus far, don't make me start at it now."

He dug his heel into Ulysses' flank and tugged on the reigns until they were once again on course. He was thankful for the glut of horsemanship that had been forced upon him in his youth before he took up his interest in acting. He scratched under his cap and shook his head. Was that him? The *real* him? Had he spent long summers riding a shining black Morgan horse through the country surrounding his family's estate?

When he was just an actor on the stage it was easy to drop his characters into a drawer at the end of the day and just be himself, but in the years since his recruitment into the Pinkerton Agency, it had become more and more difficult.

His life had grown perplexing. Every one of the handful of characters he had been forced to play as a spy constantly fought for control of his words and actions. This latest development in the war left him floating. Was there a safe place left for him, North or the South? Did Pinkerton know of his work for the Confederates? Would he be executed as a turncoat? He had failed two masters as three different people.

He was already plotting. He would become yet another person once he reached town, a person that had never had a hand in the war. Perhaps he would be a salesman. He had always enjoyed the name Xerxes. Insurance would be a fine trade. He would hail from Akron, Ohio. Chicago would be a good place for him to disappear and start again, far from the war.

Lightning crashed somewhere far off, lighting the road for miles. It ran nearly straight and he could see a few hundred yards ahead of him the rosy mist of the terrible fog that he thought he had left behind. The thunder spooked Ulysses, who tried to turn once more.

"Ho, horse!" It was harder than ever to get the horse back on track. "I'd nearly be better off walking."

A sick feeling was beginning to settle upon him. Back at the farmhouse he had played the role of Hiram the survivalist too well. Now that he had the silence to think about it, he realized that the real him would never have abandoned an old woman and a scrappy lad in the middle of Armageddon, nor would he have stolen a horse and set out in the rain to go to a potentially hostile town while the dead walked the earth.

He chewed on his lower lip. It was getting harder to keep control of the voices in his head. He pulled the horse to a stop and let the rain fall over him as he sorted out his thoughts. After a moment he nodded to himself and clicked his cheek, turning the horse around. He felt instantly better once they changed course. Ulysses seemed to step more lively and without complaint.

"I suppose you were right all along, horse." He clucked his tongue and gently squeezed Ulysses' sides. The horse sped up the best he could in the mire.

Hiram glanced behind himself every other moment and was distressed to find the mist seemed to be traveling faster than they were. He felt his hackles rise, and unslung the Spencer from beneath the oilcloth. He scanned what little he could make of his misty surroundings.

The mist was only a score of yards away. He listened intently, there was only the steady shush of the rain and the whistle of the wind that blew the drops below the bill of his cap. He blew off the moisture that was collecting on his mustache. Lightning flashed, lighting the hollow they had entered. He looked up to see the branches above his head hidden by the mist. He was in a sort of low land the mist wouldn't sink into. Something flashed by close by to the right. Ulysses grunted and began turning in a circle, stamping high splashes in a round puddle.

"Ho! Steady!" He tried to keep his rifle steady in the swirling panorama. The shadow returned to his view for one cleft second and he took a shot when he saw it. The shape dashed off before Hiram could tell if he had scored. More shades churned in the mist, and still the horse spun. Hiram acted as a dizzy turret. He opened fire on the hazy outlines as they rushed at him.

"Steady goddamn you!"

Hiram was growing weary of his revolving world. The gun-smoke he was generating made it even harder to see what he was shooting at. The world passed so quickly before his eyes he couldn't tell if he was firing upon one devil or twenty. His stomach demanded a change in its current status. He focused on keeping his lunch down and his accuracy up.

On the next rotation, a dead one flashed into view, terribly close. Just as soon as Hiram saw one blurred snatch of its muddy, noseless face it sped by before he could fire. Ulysses whinnied in the painful way only a horse could, sounding like a dozen suffering children. The horse reared, flailing its hooves as though treading water, and gave one final buck that sent Hiram up into the air.

By the time he landed ass and back into the muck the horse was nothing but a lonely whinny a thousand miles off in the mist.

Hiram took a deep breath, eating the rain and the malice that filled the ether. The jilted steps of the dead thing took up his periphery, making him roll into a puddle away from it. He groaned as he sat up, recovering the ghost that had been knocked from his chest and lamenting his soaked rifle in one utterance. He turned to the dead one and swore, half-heartedly lifted the rifle in its general direction and pulled the trigger.

Misfire. The rifle was soaked through and through.

It had been artillery, the dead one. Hiram could tell from the cut of its filthy uniform and the stumpy sword that clattered at its side. It attacked with a strange low cackle before Hiram could dodge. The tips of its fingers had worn away to sharp bony tips. They tore like the teeth of a thresher, ripping through Hiram's uniform and rending his flesh.

Hiram growled through gritted teeth and jabbed the thing in the chest with the muzzle of the rifle. It stumbled back, croaking out more of the piggish laughter. Hiram spun the rifle about in his hands, his fingers skillfully finding the notches in the barrel so it wouldn't slip from his grip. He wound up and the heavy butt of the rifle swooped through the air and let out a resounding crack against the dead soldier's skull.

Its neck cracked to the side and it spun down into the mud. In a flash Hiram was on its back, holding it in place with his knees as he unsheathed the short sword from its side. The chunky blade was sharp and heavy. In four chops the foot and a half of Union steel took the dead man's head off. Hiram jumped back from it cursing like a longshoreman.

The body still writhed on the ground, senseless arms still reaching out for him. He glanced to where the head had flopped to. It was half submerged in the water, jaw snapping open and shut, pumping the dirty water.

Hiram puzzled for a moment as he turned, tracking the movement in the mist all around him. They had always gone stone dead soon after destroying the head in some way, why did this one still move? The mist pulled in closer. It occurred to him, he had never fought the dead while inside of the mist, only while on the outskirts of it. This mist must make them more powerful the closer it is to the vile things.

He pulled the little shotgun from its holster and smiled when he saw it was dry. He cautiously took a step down the path back to the farmhouse. Nothing challenged him for a time, so he set off at the fastest trudge he could muster with all of his gear. The rain had slowed to a drizzle. The flashes of lightning were faint and the thunder was muffled as though it were a beast buried beneath the ground. At his rate it would take him hours to get back if he wasn't bothered any further. If he was lucky, perhaps he would find Ulysses grazing in a clearing a little way ahead. If he didn't recover the horse his chances of a warm reception by the old woman and the soldier were slim.

He was happy with the sword, though. Its scratched blade and dull cast brass handle looked almost pretty when the rain beaded up on its oily surface. It had a good edge, though he would take a whetstone to it the moment he had a chance to sit. Artillery men rarely used the swords in battle, but would use them to cut fuses and clear brush in great swooping chops to make way for the big guns.

It would be a silly thing to bring to a gunfight, but possibly the perfect thing against the enemy he currently faced.

His splashing tread down the rutted road was the first moment he'd had for clear thought since the madness began. He forced the gabbling voices of his other personas out of his head by humming tunes from plays he had acted in. This usually did the trick to bring him back to himself.

Despite the malice that floated in the tainted mist he walked through, he found it oddly calming- like he was hovering among the painted clouds of sunrise.

He heard the hundreds of slogging feet before they penetrated the mist. He slid into the forest. His first instinct was to run, but he stopped a short distance from the road and hid behind a stout oak. He would be hopelessly lost in the trees and mist if he let the road go too far from sight. The smell of the forest was thick and tannic with decomposing leaves. The slow drizzle filtered down through the branches high above and fell all around him, slapping the ground with the sound of a thousand roach sized snare drums.

A row of men marching six wide melted from the mist. Hiram could tell immediately that they were alive. Though they were a shambling huddled mass, they glanced all about themselves with the over-alert keenness of paranoia.

Following behind them were two small wagons, covered in tattered waxy canvas, pulled by haggard Arabian horses that weren't suited for the job.

He spied more soldiers keeping pace among the wagons and even more bringing up the rear. They were made up of all ranks; there was even a brigadier general playing teamster to one of the wagons All of them were clad in muddy wet grey. This fact quickened Hiram's breathing. The wind picked up, blowing the rain from the leaves. It made the whole forest sound alive, though the wildlife had fled at the first whiff of the ill wind.

There was a groaning creak from the chassis of the nearest wagon as it came to a stop. The brigadier thrashed the reigns, goading the thin, straining horses, but the wheels had sunk too far into the moist earth to budge. The brigadier leapt from his seat and set to cursing articulately in a way that whipped the soldiers into action, shouldering their rifles and hunkering down behind the mired wagon, counting off heaves and pushing.

Hiram wanted to use this distraction to cover his escape, but there were still a number of sharp eyed soldiers standing guard. One of them was eerily looking directly at Hiram's hiding spot, though seemingly not seeing him.

A mounted dragoon was making slow circuits of the troop. Hiram squinted in disbelief, but there was no questioning what he saw. The dragoon was riding Ulysses.

It was obvious the dark horse resisted each command, but relented before the expertly placed spurs of the horseman.

Hiram hid himself once more and listened to their grunts. He knew that he should escape as soon as he had a chance, but now that he had seen Ulysses he wasn't sure.

He had nowhere to go, he had long ago lost his bearings in the cornfield and the house was the only island of relative safety in the murky pink sea. If he returned without the horse the Irishman and the Widow would likely shoot him on sight. He couldn't leave without the horse.

The noise of the forest had grown to the point of distraction. Hiram squinted and gazed into the trees that swam in the mist. He pulled his rifle to front and cocked the hammer. The noise was not rain in the leaves. There was faint shuddering movement everywhere.

The dead were legion within the wood, gathering just out of sight.

Hiram felt his spine go straight like a scared cat's tail. He glanced at the Confederate brigade. They were oblivious to the menace and continued laboring against the stuck wagon. The dragoon had stopped circling and taken a post at the rear of the train, absently fiddling with his old musket.

A bead of sweat ran down into Hiram's eye, stinging as he blinked it away. The dead had silently begun to move toward the road by the time his vision returned. His rifle swayed between a dozen targets as yet another dozen emerged. There must have been hundreds, it sounded like more, like a muddy landslide coming slowly down a mountain.

Hiram flipped a coin in his mind and bolted before it landed.

He stuck to the trees running alongside the road. Shouts rang out among the soldiers.

"There's one now, in the trees!"

Bullets buzzed past as he ran. The undergrowth was thick, and in some places too thick to pass. It forced him closer and closer to the road. He was so close to it after twenty yards he barely had any cover.

"There's more! Jesus Christ, gunny! Get that damn repeater going! Rest of you fools aim east! Head shot or no shot!"

The forest sank to an impenetrable gully, making Hiram stop and duck behind a tree to catch his breath. They didn't seem to be firing at him anymore, though the air still cracked with their rifles and sizzled with the heat of the Gatling gun that had been uncovered on one of the wagons.

He had dodged the bullets, but he hadn't outrun the dead. Three of them tore through a bramble bush only feet away from him. The big bore pistol was in his hand, and with a pair of smoking flashes two of them hung tangled in the thorny branches with holes in their heads. The third was too fast. The thing swooped under Hiram's pistol arm and slammed him back into the tree. It was much smaller than he, but filled with such fanatical rage it was as though Hiram was being attacked by three men at once. All he could do was hook his arm over his own neck just before the ragged claws began tearing into it.

The barrel of the pistol was too long to do any good, so his hand forgot it and let it drop to the ground. He was able to hook around the horror's head and get a grip on its ear. He yanked on it like he was pulling down wallpaper. To his dismay; it peeled back the same way, taking a dripping gout of flesh away from the glistening temple.

This didn't slow it down. With one hand it tried to rip his protective arm away as the other clawed at his coat. All the while its teeth gnashed in Hiram's face, spitting rancid drool with each maniacal scream.

Hiram saw with his fingers. He saw them walking to the soft spot where the temple had been torn away. He felt his stomach churn as they probed. His untrimmed fingernails began to dig. Deeper and deeper, the meat below the muscle was softer and yielding. Three of his fingers fit in. The thing had ripped his coat, buttons flying, and he could feel the angry fingertips trying their best to squeeze into the meat between his ribs.

As his fingers penetrated deeper, Hiram could see the dead one's eyes wander and focus in different directions from one another. The assault slowed to an almost lazy pace. Hiram gritted his teeth and jammed his fingers all the way in to the third knuckle.

The dead one let out a descending moan and became weak in the knees. As it sunk, it tried to bring him down with it. Hiram brought his knee up into its chest with a hollow thump and it fell away to fidget stupidly among the leaves and twisted stumps.

Hiram spat on the damned thing and wiped its drool from his beard. A moment later he retched uncontrollably. He had unwittingly wiped his face with the hand he had just lobotomized the beast with. Before he realized his mistake, he had licked his dry, chapped lips and tasted the foul brain matter. It had reminded him of cold, rancid, bacon grease.

There was more movement in the woods, as though every branch and bough were reaching out for him. The dead were no longer silent and creeping, they were all running, climbing, jumping, screaming between the trees, while the ground writhed with those that could only crawl. Hiram took a deep breath and dashed out into the open.

Down the road the battle was still boiling. Any visibility granted by the suffuse blooming in the morning sky was obscured by billowing clouds of gun smoke, the muzzle flashes of the rifles and the unstoppable Gatling gun turning the whole scene into a thundercloud come to earth.

Nearest to Hiram, about thirty yards down the road, was the dragoon riding Ulysses. They were surrounded by three of the dead, and the horseman was barely controlling the horse's blind, bucking panic. Ulysses was backing away from each threat in clumsy circles, his hooves getting stuck in the churned up mud with each step.

The dragoon brought about a pistol and spent all six rounds in one rotation of the horse. Only one of the dead was felled by the shots. The other two that slashed at Ulysses' flank were knocked back by its crazed bulk.

The dragoon unsheathed his saber and it hung gleaming above his head for one shimmering moment before he brought it down on the shoulder of one of his foes. The blow took its outstretched arm down instantly and caught it off balance, just so. It crumpled to the ground and was pounded into the muck by frantic hooves.

The blade was back on high, not shining but crimson. On the next rotation of the spinning horse the dragoon howled and let forth a great arcing slice that found the last dead ones neck and left it behind in two pieces. The head tumbled from its gory pedestal and left the body to stand stock still for a moment until violent tremors overtook it and it fell, twisting grotesquely in the mud.

The dragoon hefted the terrible sabre above his head and cackled like the mad hessian Hiram had heard of in stories around firelight as a child.

All this time, mere seconds that took minutes to pass, Hiram had stood transfixed, recovering from his sickness in the woods, spitting unconsciously to cleanse the phantom taste from his mouth, a line of rubbery drool refusing to release his beard. Only when the third dead on dropped did he think to holster his pistol and raise his Sharps rifle. He clicked the ladder sight into place and tried to calm his breathing.

The dragoon spotted him, brought Ulysses around with a shout, and charged. Hiram breathed slow and targeted the dragoon's head. It was a difficult shot. The horse's head bobbed erratically in its gallop, blocking the horseman. Hiram was trembling minutely, not enough to be visible, but enough to cause the sight to shake off target with each breath.

The dragoon screamed, saber up and dripping. Twenty yards, then fifteen, then ten. Hiram waited for the perfect shot, but it refused to arrive. He aimed one last time, exhaled, and fired.

The dragoon's shoulder erupted and the saber dropped from his grip. He twisted in the saddle and slipped from it silently. He landed on his back five yards from Hiram, rolling back and forth and cradling his blasted shoulder.

Ulysses slowed to a canter and stopped before Hiram, who slung the Sharps back over his shoulder and stroked the horse's nose.

"Pleased to see you, again." Said Hiram, as Ulysses accepted the caress and grunted.

"He got Zeke!"

A clutch of soldiers detached from the crackling cloud of gun smoke. Hiram gave Ulysses one last pat and pulled himself up into the saddle. They charged down the road and into the mist before a shot could be fired.

# CHAPTER 18

Time had a strange way of passing now that Narcisse was buried within himself. The events at the bonfire, the implacable alien pain, they stretched like taffy that wouldn't snap. After the first of the walking dead left the circle, everything passed in a drunken blur. Vague memories of cigars smoked down to soggy nubs, burning his fingers and chapping his lips. Lingering hunger in his stomach fed only with oily burning splashes of whiskey. Narcisse's body, trying to reject all the poison. The Baron not allowing it.

Narcisse, locked in his own little suffering room. Spinning, silently screaming, feeling every ache, pain, cut, and bruise the thoughtless Loa brought upon his body. He no longer feared death, because it couldn't be any worse than the purgatory in which he floated, locked in that terrible walking coffin.

Brief glimpses fell down the well. The Baron gathering the soldiers and leading them out over the battlefield in the thickening mist. The field itself, quaking with the waking dead. The Baron giving orders without saying a word. The orders appeared to be more like pictures and feelings the Baron was able to send out to the zombi. He could feel the Loa was only in partial control of the zombi.

The zombi were the most powerful closest to Baron Samedi. They walked in columns, their movements fast and precise, but the farther away they were, the more chaos ruled. Stumbling and lashing out at one another. Wandering. Hunting.

Narcisse had seen just how terrible the army of zombi had become. In the pink morning light the morning after the attack on the Confederate camp, they surmounted a hill and the Baron had ordered two of the zombi to lift him high up on their shoulders.

The Loa had screamed in triumph causing the miles wide horde that stretched off into the mist to scream right back. Narcisse could smell the gut dropping stink, but Baron Samedi didn't seem to notice.

The Baron reached out with his mind and guided the zombi into the forest, more of a shepherd of the dead than a commander. Had Narcisse been able to shudder he would have. Every tree seemed to sway at the fetid touch of the dead.

The march through the forest had been a smear of green and brown, punctuated only by the grisly red piles left behind by those that had been caught by the zombi. Baron Samedi, endlessly smoking and drinking, laughing for no other reason than to laugh. A laugh that sounded at once like a final chapter and a pine box slamming shut.

Narcisse struggled for control. There was little else he could do. He felt if he didn't keep trying to grasp reality, what was left of him would slip away. A dull nucleus of suffering would be all that remained.

He worked in small ways, trying to move the Baron's eyes, tilt his head, wiggle a finger. When the horde surged into the cornfield, Narcisse was able to snatch control of his left hand back from the Baron. He caused it to jerk inarticulately and throw away the half smoked cigar that had been smoldering in his fingers.

The Baron immediately took the hand back. He spoke, his voice sinking into Narcisse like coffin nails.

*"Boy, sit still in there. You get the body back when I'm done with it."*

Narcisse was beaten back by each word. He tried to roll with the mental blows, ignoring the sucking pain. His mind fell back to the only comfort that was left for him.

He began to pray to the deities that had forsaken him.

*Papa Legba, Antibon Father of a Nacion Ayti,*

*The roads are covered, Papa, the paths are blocked. Only you, Papa, can clear the road.*

*Lend your hand, papa.*

Papa Legba was the gatekeeper Loa of the spirit world. Narcisse knew that if there was any chance at freedom, it was by appealing to Papa Legba.

Narcisse lost himself in this focus until they broke through the last line of corn and found that the first wave of the horde had surrounded a farm house.

The Baron calmed all of the zombi nearby with a thought and a gesture with his cigar. The starving madness of the zombi was still, and the house was a house again instead of an ant hill. He took three deep pulls from his most recent bottle and dropped it empty into a disheveled grave.

"Don't no bone move, my guedes, the Baron is thirsty."

He swaggered through a path cleared by the stinking crowd. He stood beneath the porch and slicked the rain from his ashy skin. The droplets had caused the charcoal around his eyes to drip and smear down his cheeks like a tragic Greek mask. The pupils of his eyes were so big and black they could catch flies. The whites had brown cracks running from lid to cornea, like a rotten fried egg. His unblinking eyes saw the busted windows, the smashed door. The rain had stopped and only the last few refugee drops broke the snarling half silence as they let loose from the shingles of the roof and died in the dirt.

"There's two things I need here, brethren."

He pressed the destroyed door open and walked through the kitchen, wobbling and swaying like he was on a boat in rough sea.

He stumbled against the table in the middle of the kitchen and the cast iron skillet half full with corn bread scratched off the edge and landed on the floor boards with the sound of a dirty church bell.

The Baron reached his fingers out, as though they could taste the air, and found a small cabinet. He opened it and found, behind a box of borax, a stout bottle three quarters full of clear liquid.

"Ah-hah! The first thing has been found."

He uncorked the bottle and sucked the moonshine like it was well water.

He bent over and picked up the skillet, set it down on the table, and grabbed a fist full of the pone. He shoveled the dry mash into his smiling mouth until the pan was empty and washed it down with another swig of moonshine. Another cigar was lit. His fingers momentarily flamed with spilled alcohol.

"Now, for the second thing." He thrust his hands out at hip height, palms down, and stumbled slowly through the house.

"There fertile dirt here. Yeah. The Baron need to plant a seed."

His hands began to shake when he passed over the eastern edge of the living room.

"Ah!." He spun and stumbled, catching his fall with a free hand on a chair.

"A *cellar*." He stabbed a finger at the ground.

He walked through the front door and down the porch, hands still out and shaking, and passed around the corner of the house to the cellar door. It could hardly be seen. It was covered with a pile of twitching corpses in various states of disarray. The Baron came to the pile. Kicked it with his bare foot.

"Clear these fools off. Got business inside."

The zombi that were still whole and strong set to rolling the bodies off the pile, taking bites of their burdens as they worked.

Narcisse recalled when he was young. He had done chores for the stern, but kindly, Lafitte for four years before the old man had even mentioned the zombi.

Narcisse pressed himself farther down the well within him. He remembered Lafitte's first teaching of the zombi.

\* \* \*

"The hunger of the zombi does not know living or dead, it only knows meat and blood and bone."

Young Narcisse had crouched, spellbound, with the priest that raised him after his father died. Only after hundreds of errands had the dark man began to impart the knowledge Narcisse sought, and only now, after months of menial charms and protective incantation did the elder even speak of the zombi. Narcisse's skin prickled.

"Zombi come in every shape and size and temper that man do. If a man die raging mad, thirsting for revenge in his heart, this make a mark. This all he know when he brought back." The old man drew an oval with a sharp jagged line through it in the dirt

"Calm, simple folk act like cattle when they brought back. They only wander, obey orders like sheep." He drew a square with a wave inside.

"Sad folk, they search, even if they don't know what they looking for anymore. I raised one man to work on a plantation, and his zombi wailed so bad for his mother that it was chopped for hog food after a week to keep the living slaves from goin' crazy." The elder drew a circle with a drooping line like a frown.

"There's one thing all zombi have, boy. The hunger. Every soul, no matter how happy they look in life, they got a hole in them, the need for things done but never did, things never said. When these guedes torn back into their body, all that stick with them is this great last sadness. The dead meat their guedes make move again can't fix any of these things that torture them. All that is left is the hunger. And the only thing a man cannot refuse is his stomach. Living or dead."

\* \* \*

Once the bodies were out of the way, it was clear that they weren't the only things blocking the door. There was a stout wooden shelf wedged into the rough stone entrance, gnawed and shattered by the zombi, but it still stood fast. The Baron held one hand up and gestured at the largest zombi near him.

The huge hairy man groaned and stood achingly straight at the Baron's gesture. It took a number of steps back, dug its heel into the mud, and waited.

"Hah!" The Baron swiped his hand to the obstruction and the dead man charged, growling like a bear. It launched all two hundred fifty of its pounds at the shelf, shoulder first, and crashed through with a sound like a powder keg in an outhouse.

"Nobody touch what in there, it is the Baron's now."

The hulking zombi limped from the opening, its back bent askew.

Baron Samedi picked his way through the wooden shards of the shelf down into the yawning cellar. The zombi above fell into a frenzy now that his watchful eyes weren't on them, tearing the pile of bodies to bits.

The cellar was dark except for the one puddle of pink light flowing in behind the Baron. Everything was obscured in dusty murk, save for the still body of an old woman lying on her back, arms crossed and peaceful, her wild hair interrupted where her skull had been blown out. Crucifixes where scattered around her like hayseed.

"Shame, shame, momma. Was all too much for you."

Poking into the light from the far corner of the cellar was the single scuffed toe of a bloody boot.

"Ah. Here be my soil."

The Baron stepped over the corpse and stood before the shadowed corner. The boot pulled back and receded into the shadow. Whispered mumblings floated after them.

"Get up!" The Baron boomed, raising a claw into the air.

Federal blues shuffled into the light after a whimper. The boy's eyes were unfocused and wandered like they were chasing the dust motes that danced in the column of light. His uniform was torn in several places and filthy with mud and blood. If it weren't for the faint spark that remained in his eyes he could easily be mistaken for one of the zombi. He held a broken, gore caked shovel in his hand, it dragged gratingly in the dirt behind him as he stepped forward. He looked in the Baron's direction, but didn't seem to see him.

"You're the man from the fire." His hand flexed on the shovel. "You- you did alla this." His voice was light and emotionless like a breeze blowing over the mouth of an empty bottle.

"Baron Samedi," The Baron lifted the bent top hat from his head and bowed in an overly extravagant, mocking way.

"At your *service*."

The soldier's face was still and calm, like that of a man who had lost too much blood. Silhouettes of zombi passed back and forth restlessly behind the Baron.

"I'm glad you alive, boy. I have a deal for you."

The soldier winced and blinked twice, then once slowly.

"First just you drop that spade. We gonna talk like gentleman, yes, mon ami?"

Declan's fingers strained as though they were nailed to the shattered handle, then finally snapped open and let it drop.

"This will be fast, no harm at all."

The Baron smiled with Narcisse's teeth, stained brown from the cigars.

"All the work you been laying down, mon ami, it looks like you want to live, yes?"

Declan's eyes closed and he nodded like his neck was in pain.

"Good, this will be an easy decision for you. You can either help me in life," he pointed to the shambling silhouettes outside,

"Or you can help me in death. You have to choose. I let you decide."

Declan's eyes came alive like they had thawed. They glanced between the door and the woman on the floor. His voice small and unsure.

"I want to live."

"Ah, good, good, *bon*. I'll waste no time."

The Baron took the dagger from his belt and drew it over his palm in one quick slash. His skin split and the angry gap soon welled with blood. The Baron smiled.

"Open your shirt, boy."

Declan did as he was told. His pale skin was pocked with goose bumps.

Without any warning, Baron Samedi swung and cut a foot long gash from Declan's clavicle to his ribs. Declan's mouth snapped open and he trembled, a cry frozen in his chest.

"Be still. This gonna hurt."

The Baron pumped his bleeding hand three times and held it to Declan's wound. Declan's whole body jerked and he froze, arms up like he was crucified. Outside, the zombi were wailing. The Baron's teeth clenched, the ropes of his neck stood taut. The dead cigar hanging from the corner of his lips came to life with a brilliant cherry ember.

Narcisse saw all this through the Baron's eyes, but within himself he saw other things. He saw a glowing red channel cut across the darkness, slithering in waves like a hot, iron snake. It came from the pin-spot of white light. He felt it climb up the chest, through the arm, and burst out of the wound.

The energy pulsed into Declan, who was petrified in that painfully hung position, twitching like his body couldn't handle the influx. The Baron spoke to Declan, though Narcisse didn't hear it come from his mouth, the Loa was communicating directly to the soldier's soul.

*I'm plantin' a seed in you, boy. A little piece of me, the gro-bon-ange. It gonna grow little by little. Nothin' you can do about that. I'll always be able to talk with you like this, now. You wonderin' why I do this, yes? I need a body to stay on this side of the spirit world, and they don't last too long when I in them. I can't just jump from body to body, people have to invite me in, and their soul has to be weak enough to let me take over.*

The Loa laughed, a terrible feeling to have in your head, like something gnawing at the inside of Declan's skull.

*So, I plant my seed in you, Declan. When this body give up in a little while, I pop over to you and move on in. We tied together now, yes? We bound, so don't try killin' me, won't do no good. I'm with you forever, mon ami. Don't go gettin' yourself killed either. You gonna be stronger now, but you ain't invincible. You not special. Soon as I find somebody else I can plant I'm going to. More seeds I have out there, the longer I can stick around this side.*

The Loa began to withdraw from Declan's mind.

*Maybe I see you again someday. Maybe I be you? Ha! Look after that body for me...*

Declan was released from the paralytic grip and sunk to his knees. He toppled over with a groan.

"Sleep well, little seed."

The Baron wiped the dagger clean on his pant leg and climbed the stairs out into the yard.

"Let's be lively brethren!" He bellowed. "We got a long march ahead!"

Narcisse returned to begging the other Loa for help as the horde marched forever northward. He thought of the great cities of the north. Cities with more dead in their cemeteries than living above ground. He felt, he *knew*, that something far more terrible than what had already happened lay just over the horizon.

# CHAPTER 19

Hiram could smell the sweet water of the creek, flowing swiftly enough to wash away the filth that had passed through it. He wanted more than anything to crawl through the mud beneath the bridge and drink deeply from the flow. His canteen was long missing, probably torn from its strap by a tree branch during one of his many sprints through the forest. Behind him the horse's flank rose and fell with comforting regularity, warmth radiating off of him like some huge hot water bottle.

They had been lucky to find the bridge just before the army of the dead overtook them. The riverbank had a gentle enough slope for them to clamber off the road and squeeze themselves in the wedge of dryish clay between the stout pilings. Minutes later the horde caught up and started crossing the river, the legion of their footfalls sounding like a rain of stones on an unsound roof.

They didn't only cross at the bridge, but waded through the wide shallow river as far as Hiram could see. The damned mist had served to protect the two of them as they shivered under the bridge. Though thousands of the terrible things shambled down the bank and splashed clumsily through the formerly pristine water, none of them noticed Hiram. He slowly stroked the horse's mane to calm it, but it was unnecessary. Ulysses had either grown used to the perpetual terror that life had become, or it was too exhausted to kick up a fuss.

Hiram was numbly tired as well, not feeling alive so much as living. He fought to keep his eyes open and alert for over an hour as the dead streamed by. He drifted off as the boot-falls above thinned out, an almost relaxing sound if you didn't know what was making it.

It was the sound of a single set of boots that woke him. When the boots had been many the wall of noise had been a strange lullaby, but now that there was only the 'trump-trump' of one body pacing above, it felt infinitely more sinister.

Hiram ran his hand down Ulysses' flank. The horse was still dead to the world. He drew and checked the works of his revolvers. They had stayed dry beneath his coat; he wouldn't trust his life to the rifles until he had a chance to clean them. He stripped off his extra gear and slowly edged around the piling.

He paused and listened once he reached the edge of the overhang. He was still. Listening. Planning. The boots had stopped above. He flexed the grips of the pistols, slick with machine oil and the sweat from his nervous palms. The creek. The creek babbled on.

A brown gout of liquid jetted from above and plunked into the river. He watched where the gob had landed. It spread out tendrils in the flow, brown leaking off of it like wet smoke. Tobacco spit. Dead men don't chew tobacco.

Hiram was relieved for a moment until he realized that, alone as he was, a living man with a gun could be far more dangerous than a dead one. He tried to twist his head up to catch a glimpse of a boot or a cuff overhanging the bridge for some little clue as to whether the man above was friend or foe, but he couldn't get a good enough angle without exposing himself.

He decided to make an enemy of the unknown. Ulysses was still asleep, ear twitching, as Hiram passed by, slouching and picking silent footing to the other side of the bridge. He didn't hear the boots move, but the flow of the river was just loud enough to wash out the finer parts of his ears.

He waited for any sound telling where his prey lay, but felt nothing.

Crab-walking carefully, he clinged close to the frame of the bridge, feeling the same nervous excitement that churned up in his gut as a younger man, sneaking out of his parent's home for no other reason than to walk the moonlit cobbles and know he was the only soul awake. On those walks he had always fancied death to be shining his sickle just around the corner in every alley. It filled him with a delicious terror, even though he was protected by the intangible iron-cladding of youth. Now, despite how he carried himself, he knew for a fact that death was lurking in every grass-lot, cupboard, and cave. In the glinting eye of a beautiful woman, really just the gleam of that terrible blade. Her smile. Just a showing of teeth.

Had he been raised in Boston? Had he walked the streets at night? He wished for a moment, just before he poked his head above the bridge, that he would have a few days to himself when this was all over so that he could find out who he truly was. It was beginning to get hard to breathe beneath all the lies.

He spun and popped up, half covered by the thick railing of the bridge.

It was easily five yards off, what he saw, but it was unmistakable. The negative, darker than black circle of a rifle barrel, rimmed with the crescent shine of well-oiled blue steel.

That pretty lady winked at Hiram as he dove down into the stony clay.

Of course, he thought, you got caught by surprise. You're an actor, not a soldier.

Splinters of wood were in the air where Hiram's head had only just been.

The slug had not struck his body, but as he lay were he landed, gasping, he felt as though every grain of it had passed through him.

He let himself slide and roll down the slick pitch, all the while hearing those steadfast boots knocking on the planks of the bridge like a well-timed hammer falling. Hiram could not tell where the boots were headed. The wash of the stream and the echo of the underbridge made the thump of the phantom heels huge and amorphous things.

He did not know if they had made for the nearest rail, to fire down upon him, or if they headed round the entry of the bridge to pursue him. He was now hunted.

He forced his roll to a stop just as he reached the pilings and glanced at his revolvers. In his chaotic spin they had slapped against the living dirt enough to make it look as though they had been dug from a balsa wood casket. He crawled and hid behind a piling, swatting at the mud that caked the firearms. There wasn't any escape. He had succeeded against the odds thus far and knew only a fool would tease fate an inch farther than he had.

Instantly cold, all of his nervous heat turned liquid, coating his body. So thick and rich, he could smell his own fear. There was so much mud clogging each and every opening of his pistols he would have better luck chucking skipping stones at his adversary.

There weren't even any stones around to speak of.

He crouched behind the piling, choking the useless lumps of iron like it meant something; listening for bootfalls that wouldn't arrive, maybe the crunch of gravel underfoot. The betrayer nature made everything moist and silent, reducing every sound until it was aqueous. The rain, the river. The damned fog. All of it water.

*"Blast it, let's go."*

Hiram swung around the piling and pointed up the bank where he imagined the hunter to be, both slimy brown pistols brandished. He even started to scream.

What he saw:

The crescent. Gleam on the tube. Bitter black. A color that ran through him even before the smart rifle took its shot. The smallest nod of the unfocussed shaggy head behind the gun.

Hiram's body did the rest. The rifle sounded like a wreath being hammered indelicately to a shabby door. His head, shoulders, they had snapped back behind the piling; but the trip was a long one. He saw the river scroll past as he dodged, stinking now with gore at her edges. He knew whatever ripples man made on her surface would soon be forgotten.

The taint of the thousand score dead men that dragged their carcasses through her were no more than a speck of dust, lost in the eye of the world after a single unconscious blink.

Hiram gasped behind the temporary safety of the piling. There was no way a bullet could get him out of the situation. He was tired of fighting, even more tired of running. He gave up.

"Cease fire!"

His voice sounded foreign in his ears, he tasted the desperation as the words left his mouth. He hadn't played a looser since back at the play-house, a hundred years ago and a half dozen lives past.

Nothing could be heard but the erasing hush of the river and Ulysses, awakened by the shots, scuffing at the dirt, trying to get out of the position it had wedged itself into. He waved at the horse in an effort to calm him, but Ulysses took it as a queue to come on over. Hiram shooed the horse, to no effect. He could hear feet carefully trudging down the bank. All bravery shivered off of Hiram.

"Cease fire!" He yelped again. "I've got a horse under here!"

The steps stopped.

The water-sound.

"Are you threatening me with a horse?" Called out a low, thick voice.

The voice reminded Hiram of something that the panic of his mind couldn't grab ahold of. He tried to answer but the words hooked the back of his throat and he coughed in a fit. Ulysses regained his hooves and nudged him tenderly.

"No, no, I-"

"Throw those pistols out here were I can see 'em and step out hands first. *Slow*."

The pistols landed in the clay with heavy thumps and Hiram walked from behind the piling, arms out like a man blinded. The man was halfway down the bank; the rifle stared down. He made a noise almost like a laugh.

"Well, shit. Didn't recognize you without that arsenal strapped to your back."

The rifle swooped down from the man's face, and Hiram felt the tension in him shoot off someplace far away. He dropped his hands and stood slack jawed.

"*Hobb*? You made it out of the ambush."

"Can't say the same for the rest. You been dodgin' all these ghouls what've gotten so popular?"

Hobb tugged the drooping bandana that covered his face back into place.

"C'mon, let's get that horse up where it's dry."

Hobb was slurring his S's. Hiram had never heard him do that before. There wasn't a thing on Hobb that would pass muster. His uniform was torn like he had gotten between a wild-cat and her cubs. Stained three shades of crimson brown, blood ranging from nearly new and wet to crusty flakes, holding on in the way only blood can.

The three of them trundled up the hill. Hiram noticed that it looked like Hobb had lost the ring and pinky finger on his right hand. The good fingers and thumb doomed forever to mimic a gun. Hiram rubbed at the filthy cloth covering the gash on his neck. It was the kind of wound that grew hot and itched terribly, but made you sorry when you gave it what it wanted.

The rush from his showdown with Hobb was gone and every ache, pain, cut, and strain began to throb to the beat of every other step. If for any reason but to drown out how wretched he felt, Hiram made himself talk. He could still taste brain matter if he wasn't careful where he put his tongue.

"I've been running since I last saw you." They'd made it up the bank and clopped with Ulysses up onto the bridge. They were out in the open, nowhere to take cover, but when their eyes met for half a moment, it seemed there was a nonverbal agreement that they were both too tired to care.

"How did you get by, Hobb?"

"At least up here we can see what's coming."

Hobb held his head at an odd angle and spat a brown jet of tobacco juice over the edge into the river. They didn't hear it land.

Hiram repeated himself. "How have you been getting on since we parted ways?"

Hobb looked to Hiram, his eyes even more piercing when punctuated by the bandanna. He lifted the wrap a bit a spat awkwardly from beneath it. He looked far off, as though he could contemplate the waves of the far off ocean.

"Shit, we're both men, right? Suppose I should show you."

He pulled the knot loose on the bandanna and pulled it away slowly. The fabric crinkled and cracked as it came off, plucking away bits of dried gore and scabs as it left.

Hiram stifled a gasp and only nodded solemnly at the portrait before him. Hobb's cheek looked like it had been lanced with a fish-hook, but the angler that had speared him had gotten anxious and pulled back too hard. His jaw was torn from back where his molars bit down up to the front, the lower lip unconnected and hanging.

"Don't want to talk about how I got this."

He tied the bandanna back into place.

"Don't want to talk about much of anything. We should keep moving."

Hiram stepped to Hobb and slapped him in the back, much like he would a widower at a funeral.

"You can ride the horse." Hiram said.

"I don't need no goddamn horse." Hobb spat again, uncontrolled, it dribbled down the filthy bandanna. "I don't need you, either."

Hobb pulled away from Hiram and fell into a northward march, the direction the dead had traveled.

"Let's go! Move! We're losing daylight..." His heel came down wrong on a broken plank and he twisted down until his splayed face scraped the dust of thousand boot heels that covered the bridge.

"Shitfire!" He bellowed, "Hell above! I don't know where I'm going!"

Hobb was crying, huge terrifying bursts like a bear in a trap. It was so unnatural it made Hiram sick with fear to see it.

Of all the men he had met, Hobb was the only one he had imagined could march through every layer of hell and back and have nothing but a worn pair of boots to complain about. All at once, everything felt more terrible, impossible, and desperate.

Hiram pulled the laces tight on his sanity, sealing as much of the last few days from his mind as he could. This wasn't the end of the world. The dead did not walk. It was not ridiculous to try and fight the unending wall of hungry flesh that fate had brought before them. For that moment, they were only two men and a horse, hoping to stay alive in a world that made as little sense as it ever had. He knelt by Hobb and shook him until the older man's wild eyes found focus.

"Hobb! I don't know where to go, but I know where we *can* go."

"Where! There can't be any place left for the living..." Hobb stopped and held his head. He looked at Hiram as though he were a stranger.

"There may be one. I know the way." Hiram tugged the stolen map from his inner pocket and smoothed it on the planks of the bridge.

"There's a farmhouse not too far..."

"That's, that's one of Wrathbone's maps.." Hobb was silent, his wrinkled brow knitting. "You..."

Hobb shoved Hiram, sending him stumbling back a half dozen steps until his back was to the guardrail of the bridge.

"All your sneakin' around. You're the one that gave away our position. You stayed back so you wouldn't get hit."

Hobb's rifle whirled through the air and its butt cracked Hiram across the jaw. Ulysses started and reared up with a whinny that spooked a nearby crow from the thistle branch it had been watching them from. As easy as breathing Hobb had the rifle aimed directly between Hiram's eyes.

"You rotten, no good, *spy*."

# CHAPTER 20

The crow jolted at the whinny of the horse and rose quickly at first, until it found a warm updraft that it rode with a gentle curve of its wings.

Up and up, it rode the draft in larger circles, following the hunger that forever drove it. Back down, it coasted away from the sun, down to the clearing where there were sometimes things to eat. It dove down, calling to see if there were others like him there, but there was no reply.

It looked like there were piles of food everywhere, but each pile it hopped to had a strange smell like dirt or old waste. It called once more and something called back. There was a man on his knees amidst these strange untouchable piles, he was screaming over and over, but not in any way that made sense to the crow. It hopped carefully toward the screaming man. It had the smell of death on it as well, but it wasn't like the inedible sour smell of the carrion. The crow thought the man might be dying, and this excited it.

It followed the man as he stumbled senselessly around the yard. The man came to a pile of bodies near the house, where the woman used to sometimes scatter grain. He crawled to the pile and began throwing bodies off of it, as though he were digging for something.

The man found a mangled body that was different from the others. It was a female; the parts of it that were untorn were soft and smooth. A very small human was clutched in its arms. The man began to make sounds very much like a crow cawing. The crow responded in kind and hopped along at a safe distance as the man dragged the strange bodies around to the yard by the corn. The man's crowing grew to be so wild and startling that the crow took to the air and circled above in safety.

The man brought the bodies to a rough hole in the ground and rolled them into it. He was silent as he covered them over with soil. Once the job was done, he clasped his hands together and bent over on his knees, head to the dirt. The man's back heaved up and down while he made noises like a very sick animal.

The crow was restless. It would look for food elsewhere and return later to see if the man had died yet. From how things looked, it wouldn't be long.

It circled up and up, as high as the drafts would carry it. The rising sun was glinting on its right wing as it flew North, past the river where it usually fed. A short way after the river it ran into the fog that had confounded it the night before. It cawed dejectedly and turned around. There would be no food in there, only more masses of the sour, inedible things. The fog spread out farther than any cloud it had ever seen. From high up, the only things visible were a chain of hills popping above the soupy pink, like the knuckles of a fist held just above water.

It descended and landed on the weathervane of the house, motionless in the stagnant morning. The man was silent now. There was another body with him in the yard, this one untwisted and smelling freshly dead. He dug into the turf next to the first burial. He paused from time to time to look at the sky and mutter.

The crow settled down to wait. The crow was good at waiting.

## About the Author

Brenton Harper-Murray lives in Chicago. After getting numerous short stories published, he decided to turn one of them into a novel after a beautiful woman told him she kind of liked it. Brenton maintains a blog at poorbrenton.com and you can follow his demented ramblings on Twitter @poorbrenton

Brenton would like to thank the following amazing people (in no particular order) that backed the Kickstarter that funded the first printing of this book. This wouldn't be possible without you.

Corinne Halbert, Erica Polacek, Patricia Foltz, Patty Sue Fanella, Frank Wuerbach, James Stuart, Carlene Bruno, Tanner Smith, Katina Vastlik, Christopher Papineau, Carlee Weimer, Feather Metsch, Janet Gatz, Steve Chamberlin, Evan Haberecht, Lyn Harper, Clive Patmore, Angela Ratkovich, Dale Price, Alice, Morton Weir, Arnie Bernstein, Kate Madison, Yuan Song, Elizabeth Harper-Allen, Everett Gonzalez, Roland Bashnack, Paul, Sonia Koval, Ann Harper, Brian Beirne, John Jesse Houlihan, Kevin Murray, Brooke O'Neil, Craig Hackl, Aaron House, Alisha Jones, Lyrael, Frank Johnson Sr., Kylene Simek, Raina Kellerman, Robert Banning, Lauren Price, Elisabeth Kehler, Matthew Feimer, Teel McClanahan III, Allan Cardenas, Vicki Graves, Kelly Koch, Kirk Finley, Debbi Pantaleo, Marcia Welch, Matt Steel, Rosemary Bidun, Pierick Smith, Justin Zerza, Amanda Holt, Adam Witt, Greg X. Graves, Joseph Grzelak, Charly Sparks, and Bobby Allen.